SNEAK PEEK EXCERPT FROM

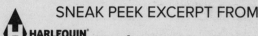

HARLEQUIN®

KISS™

WHAT THE BRIDE DIDN'T KNOW

"I can't find my honeymoon nightie. Do you have it?"

Trig opened his mouth as if to speak and then shut it again with a snap. He shook his head. *No.*

She looked beneath the pillows. "Did we rip it?"

Still no sound from Trig.

"Could be the cleaner mistook it for ribbon," he said at last.

"Ribbon?"

"There wasn't much of it. But there were bows. Lots of bows. Made out of ribbon."

"Oh." Lena tried to reconcile ribbon nightwear with the rest of her clothing. "I really should be able to remember that."

She passed her husband on the way to the shower and when she stepped beneath the spray she could have sworn she heard him whimper.

DEAR READER,

There's a moment in every friends-to-lovers story where *someone* has to fess up to being in love with the other person. It's a moment laced with courage and fraught with peril. What if you lose your best friend? The one who's been there for you since kindergarten? The one who's already so entwined in your life that losing them would snap you like a kite string in a vicious wind?

That's the starting point for Lena and Trig in *What the Bride Didn't Know*. I added foreign lands, danger, concussion, mystery, soul baring, protectiveness and betrayal. I added love, deep and abiding, and fell in love with my hero along the way.

There's a short enovella to accompany this story, *The Night Before Christmas...*, available from www.Harlequin.com in December, and it gives us a snapshot of Lena and Trig's relationship when they were just out of their teens. Oh, the tension! The cluelessness. The angst! The novella also follows the story of Jess Turner—an old girlfriend of Trig's—who returns to the sleepy seaside town she grew up in with one clear goal in mind: this Christmas, she'll show bad boy Boyd Webber what a fool he was to ever have let her go.

I hope you enjoy the stories.

Happy reading!

Kelly Hunter

www.KellyHunter.net

WHAT THE BRIDE DIDN'T KNOW

KELLY HUNTER

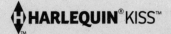

Recycling programs
for this product may
not exist in your area.

ISBN-13: 978-0-373-20737-4

WHAT THE BRIDE DIDN'T KNOW

Copyright © 2013 by Kelly Hunter

www.Harlequin.com

ABOUT KELLY HUNTER

Accidentally educated in the sciences, Kelly Hunter has always had a weakness for fairy tales, fantasy worlds and losing herself in a good book. Husband... yes. Children...two boys. Cooking and cleaning...sigh. Sports...no, not really—in spite of the best efforts of her family. Gardening...yes. Roses, of course. Kelly was born in Australia and has traveled extensively. Although she enjoys living and working in different parts of the world, she still calls Australia home.

Kelly's novels *Sleeping Partner* and *Revealed: A Prince and a Pregnancy* were both finalists for a Romance Writers of America RITA® Award in the Best Contemporary Series Romance category!

Visit Kelly online at www.kellyhunter.net.

Other Harlequin® KISS™ titles by Kelly Hunter:
The One That Got Away

This and other titles by Kelly Hunter are available in ebook format—check out **Harlequin.com.**

For my mother, grandmother, aunt, children, Anne, Trish, Carol, Fi, Meredith, Lissa, Linda, Barb, Rosie and Jo. Thanks for all your support.

WHAT THE BRIDE DIDN'T KNOW

PROLOGUE

Seventeen-year-old Lena West didn't understand the question. It had something to do with Euler's formula and complex z but, beyond that, Lena had no clue. Groaning, she dropped her pen on top of her grid paper and put her palms to her eyes so that she couldn't see the sweep of ocean beyond the screen door. Summer and school work never mixed well. Not when there was a beach a few metres from the house and a swell that had seen her older brother take to the water the minute they'd arrived home from school.

It wasn't fair that Jared could do his maths homework in his head. It didn't help that her two *younger* siblings were bona-fide geniuses—one evil and one not—and could have answered question six in under ten seconds. Fourteen-year-old Poppy—who was not evil—would have helped her had she been around, but Poppy had been seconded to the University of Queensland's mathematical think tank and spent most of her time in Brisbane these days. Thirteen-year-old Damon wasn't around to ask either. He was pulling yet another after-school detention—his theory being that if he was unruly enough and sneaky enough, he might just manage to avoid the land of secret-squirrel think thanks altogether. Lena applauded Damon's initiative, even if she didn't like his chances.

When you were that bright, people noticed.

Not that Lena had anything to worry about there.

Sighing, Lena opened her eyes and picked up her pen. Question six. There it was. Mocking her. One simple little question that everybody else in her freaky family could do in their sleep.

'Moron,' she grumbled.

'Who is?' said a deliciously deep voice from behind her and Lena nearly slipped her skin because she hadn't heard anyone come in. She knew the voice though, and her scowl deepened as she turned to glare at Adrian Sinclair, their neighbour from two doors down and Jared's best friend since kindergarten. 'Don't you *knock*?' she asked grumpily and knew it for a stupid question even as it left her mouth. Adrian didn't have to knock—he practically lived here.

'Didn't want to interrupt your thought flow.'

'And yet, you did.'

Adrian's grin kicked sideways. 'You said "moron". I thought you were talking to me.'

'Moron.'

'See what I mean?'

Hard not to smile right along with Adrian's laughing brown eyes. 'Smiling crooked will get you no-where.'

'That's not always true. Jared around?'

'Out there.' Lena nodded towards the Pacific. It was still blue. It still beckoned. Jared was heading out of the water, board in hand. 'Why aren't you out there with him?'

'Thinking about it,' said Adrian. 'Why aren't you?'

'I have a maths test tomorrow.' Lena eyed him speculatively. Adrian had chosen the same school subjects that Jared had. Same subjects she'd chosen, give or take a language or two. He and Jared were a year ahead of her in school. 'What do you know about Euler's formula and complex planes?'

Adrian moved closer, edging in over her shoulder. 'Which question's giving you trouble?'

'Six.'

'The bonus question? You know you can always leave it?'

'How about we pretend that's not an option?' It wasn't. Not in this household.

'All right.' Adrian reached for her textbook and started flipping through it as if he actually knew what he was looking for. Long wrists. Big hands like pad-dles. Thick, strong fingers with callouses that came of hours spent kite surfing. Lena had the insane urge to put her palm against his and take measure, note down exactly how warm and big and rough those hands of his were...

And then the textbook thunked down on the table

beside her, and Adrian's chest brushed her shoulder as he pointed to a particular section of text, and...*damn* but it was getting hot in here.

'You want a chair?' she asked, the better to put some breathing distance between them.

'Been sitting all day. 'M good.'

Lena shifted restlessly and got a nose full of Adrian's body-scent for her trouble. He smelled spicy clean, tantalisingly fine—and this after an afternoon of school sport. As if he'd taken the time to shower before heading over here, which made no sense at all given his tendency to end up in the ocean regardless.

'So...' he prompted, his voice gruffer than usual. 'Question six.'

Right. Question six. Lena dragged her attention back to the matter at hand. No! Not the hands! Question six. 'So I tried to find a—'

'What's going on?' said a voice from the patio doorway, and she knew every nuance of that voice too, no need to look up to know that Jared was standing in the doorway or that he'd be wearing a scowl.

She looked up anyway and met her brother's narrowed gaze with curiosity. He had unruly black hair—a trait they shared, although hers was considerably longer and considerably more unruly. He had bluer eyes than she did because hers often tended towards grey in the right kind of light. They both had athletic builds. Lena had a yearning for curves, but it wasn't going to happen. She had a scowl just like the one Jared was wearing. The family resemblance was strong.

'What's wrong with you? Not enough Jared West groupies on the beach?' Jared was a wanted man as far as the girls around here were concerned. Most of those girls made friends with Lena in order to get closer to him, which wasn't a problem except that Jared changed girlfriends with dazzling speed and not many of them stayed friends with Lena afterwards.

'Their loss,' Jared had told her when she'd complained about the defection of her friends, and, while his curt words had soothed her ego, the fact remained that Lena was still appallingly low on company because of him. Jared had been more inclined to let her tag around with him after that, probably out of pity.

Lena could have done without the pity, but beggars couldn't be choosers.

'I *said*, what are you doing?' repeated Jared, heavy on the ice.

'Trig,' said Lena, figuring a straight answer might appease him.

Jared's gaze shifted to Adrian. 'That what she's calling you these days?'

Adrian held Jared's bleak gaze with an enigmatic one of his own. 'If something's bothering you, J, spit it out.'

Jared's gaze shifted between her and Adrian once more. Adrian straightened slowly and some message flashed between him and her brother that Lena didn't have the cipher for.

'You know the rules,' said Jared curtly.

'Do I know the rules?' she asked. 'What rules?'

'He thought I was hitting on you,' said Adrian, after another long and loaded silence. 'It's not encouraged.'

'*Excuse* me?' said Lena. There were two issues buried in that simple little statement, and while her mind shied away from the implication that Adrian might actually *like* her enough to hit on her, it had no trouble whatsoever grappling with the second. 'Jared *West*, are you scaring away my potential boyfriends? Because if you are...and I find out you are...' Lena narrowed her gaze. 'Is this why Ty Chester didn't ask me to the year eleven dance? Because he was going to—I know he was. And then he *didn't*.'

'Nah, that one was all you,' said Jared. 'He probably thought you were going to ask him hang-gliding in return. I hear he's scared of heights.'

'And kittens,' added Adrian. 'Possibly his own shadow.'

'Maybe I was after a refreshing change,' she grumbled. 'Maybe I *wanted* to see how the quiet, handsome half lived.' Facts were facts. Ty Chester *was* uncommonly handsome. Nor would it have killed her to spend some time with people she *hadn't* hero-worshipped since birth.

'You'd have eaten him alive,' said Jared.

'Yes, that was the plan. Jared, I swear, if I ever catch you interfering in my love life I will make your love life a living hell. Yours too,' she told Adrian for good measure.

'Mine's already a living hell,' murmured Adrian and Jared snorted. More silent communication passed between them, effectively cutting her out of the loop. They did it all the time and mostly it didn't bother her. Today, it did.

'Lord, you two, get a room.'

'Yeah, *Trig*,' said Jared, darkly gleeful. 'Let's get a room.'

'If we go surfing this afternoon, I'm going to drown you,' said Trig, formerly known as Adrian.

Jared flipped him a friendly finger.

'Is this foreplay?' asked Lena. 'Because if it is, can it happen elsewhere? I'm trying to concentrate on my homework here.' A valid point as far as she was concerned. Unfortunately, it focused Jared's attention back on her books.

'Since when do you need help with maths homework?' he asked.

'Since it got hard. What kind of idiot question is that?'

'Seriously? You really can't do basic trigonometry?'

'This is why I don't think I'm fully related to any of them,' Lena told Adrian. 'I'm the milkman's baby.'

'Yeah, baby, but you've got a lot of grit,' offered Adrian. 'Who cares if it takes you a fraction longer than the rest of them to figure out a trigonometry proof? You'll still get there.'

'Yeah, but not fast enough. And then they'll disown me. That's what happens to people who can't keep up.'

'Since when have you ever not kept up?' This from

Jared who'd never had to work to keep up with anything. He was always out front; always the leader. And Lena had always worked her butt off to make sure that she wasn't that far behind.

It was costing her, though. More and more, she could feel the gap between what her siblings could do and what she could do widening. It was the curse of being an ordinary person in an extraordinary family.

'Would you disown me if I did fall behind?' she asked.

And shocked Jared speechless.

Adrian was looking at her funny—as if he'd known all along that her insecurities were there but he couldn't quite figure out why she was voicing them now. Lena didn't know why she was voicing them now either. It was just a maths question.

'Never mind,' she said awkwardly.

'You won't fall behind.' Jared had finally found his voice. 'I won't let you.'

He just didn't get it. 'But what if that's where I'm meant to be? Water finding its own level, and all that?'

'No,' said Jared grimly. 'The hell with that. That's just defeatist.'

'No one's leaving anyone behind,' said Adrian soothingly. 'No one here's defeated. Jared's never going to disown you, Lena. He's insanely protective of you. Did you not just see him go caveman on my arse for daring to look at you sideways?'

'Sure I did,' said Lena. 'But he's protecting *you*, not me.'

'Maybe I'm protecting you both,' said Jared. 'Anyone ever think of that?'

'Overachiever,' murmured Lena and Adrian nodded his agreement, and it made Lena laugh and broke the tension and she was all for it staying broken.

'How about I start this conversation again?' she offered.

'Can you do it without the emo infusion?' asked Jared.

'You want the bare basics?' She could do that. She pointed the pen at her chest. 'Imbecile in need of a little help with her maths homework, before *she* can go surfing. I'm stuck on question six.'

Which was how Lena scored *two* maths tutors for the rest of the year and how Adrian Sinclair earned the nickname Trig.

Nothing to do with being trigger happy at all.

Even if he was.

ONE

It wasn't easy being green. Green being the colour of envy. Envy being the emotion Lena owned when she saw others walking around effortlessly and without pain. She tried to keep her resentments in check, but envy had powerful friends like self-pity and unfocused anger and when *they* came to play, Lena's bright-side surrendered with barely a murmur. Being gut shot nineteen months ago had brought out the worst in her rather than the best.

Focus on the positives, the overworked physio had told her briskly at the start of her rehabilitation.

You're alive.

You can walk.

The physio had tapped the side of Lena's skull next. You're really strong. Up here.

Lena had taken that last comment as a compliment. Right up until the physio had started telling her to back off on the exercises and let her body heal. Lena had ignored her, at which point the physio had started comparing Lena to someone's pet ox.

As in overly stubborn and none too bright.

It didn't help that the other woman might possibly have been right.

Still, stubbornness had got her to the airport this morning, and through the airport, and if she sank down into the row of seats next to the boarding gate with a muffled curse and a certain amount of relief, so what?

She'd made it.

Another half an hour and she'd be on a plane bound for Istanbul and when she got there she was going to find Jared, her wayward brother, and haul him home in time for Christmas. She could do this. *Was* doing this.

Didn't matter that she was doing it one step at a time.

Lena closed her eyes and rubbed at her face, putting the heels of her hands to her eye sockets and rolling them in slow circles, and it was hell on mascara but she didn't wear any anyway—her lashes were black enough and thick enough to go without. Her hair was thick and black too, and straight these days, on account of a good cut and a run-in with a hair straightener this morning. The wave would come back next time she washed it, but for now she looked reasonably put together. Less like an invalid and more like a woman on a mission.

Someone took a seat beside her and Lena lowered

her hands, cracked a glance and groaned at the sight of her nemesis, Adrian Sinclair, glaring back at her.

Trig was big. As in six feet five and perfectly proportioned. He'd grown into his hands. Grown into the coat-hanger shoulders he'd had at sixteen. Good for him.

Lena had stopped growing at a respectable five-eight. Nothing wrong with medium height. Nothing wrong with medium anything.

'Go away,' she said by way of greeting.

'No,' he said by way of hello. 'I heard you failed your physical.'

Way to rub it in. 'I'll take it again. I've put in for special consideration.'

'You won't get it.'

'You're blocking it?'

'You overestimate my influence,' rumbled Trig. 'Lena—'

'No,' she said, cutting him off fast. 'Whatever you're going to say about my current state of well-being, *don't*. I don't want to hear it.'

'I know you don't, but I am *done* talking around it.' Trig's jaw tightened. He had a nice jaw. Strong. Square. It provided a much-needed counterpoint to his meltingly pretty brown eyes. 'When are you going to get it through your thick head that you are never going to get your old job back?'

Lena said nothing. Not what she wanted to hear.

'Doesn't mean you can't be equally effective elsewhere,' continued Trig doggedly.

'Behind a *desk*?'

'Operations control. Halls of power. Could be fun.'

'If it's that much fun, why don't *you* do it?'

'What do you think I've been *doing* these past nineteen months? Besides dropping everything on a regular basis to come babysit you? Why do you think I took myself off rotation in the first place?'

Lena had the grace to flush. Like her and Jared, Trig had been part of an elite intelligence reconnaissance team once, and, just like her, Trig had loved his job. The extreme physicality of it. The danger and the excitement. The close calls and the adrenaline. Trig *had* to be missing all that. 'Why *did* you take yourself off rotation? They'd have assigned you to another team. No one asked you to sit at a desk. And I *don't* need a babysitter.'

'Yeah, I wish you'd prove it.' Trig eased his legs out in front of him and tried to make himself comfortable in the too-small airport seat. Big man, with a body honed for combat. The pretty face and the easy smile...those were just for disarmament purposes.

'Adrian, what are you doing here?' Adrian was his real name. Lena only ever used it when talk turned serious. 'How'd you even know I was here?'

'Damon called me. He had you flagged the minute you passed through Customs.'

'Man, I hate that.' Who'd have a computer hacker for a brother? 'No respect for privacy whatsoever.'

'Handy, though. Exactly what is it you plan to do in Istanbul, Lena?'

'Find Jared.'

'What makes you think he's still there?'

'I don't. But it's the only lead we've got. Nineteen months and not one word on his whereabouts until now. What if he needs our help?'

'If he needs our help he'll ask for it.'

'What if he can't? Jared's in over his head. I can feel it. He wouldn't go this long without finding a way to contact us. He just wouldn't.'

'He would if he thought the risk of blowing his cover was too great.'

'If it's that dangerous, maybe he shouldn't be there at all.'

Trig shrugged. 'Jared wants answers. He *needs* answers. Get in his way and he's not going to be happy.'

'I won't get in his way. You give me too little credit.'

'I have never given you too little credit. That's not a mistake I'm likely to make. Too much *leeway,* on the other hand...'

'Misogynist.'

'Not even close.'

'So you *don't* plan to sling me over your shoulder and forcibly remove me from the boarding area?'

'Too showy,' said Trig, pulling out his mobile phone and tapping the screen. A nerve twisted low in Lena's belly and she shifted restlessly in her seat and looked away. She'd always had a thing for Trig's hands. A little part of her had long wondered what they might wring from her if Trig ever put his mind to it.

Not that he ever did.

'We took a vote; me, Damon and Poppy,' Trig continued. 'In the event that I can't persuade you to stay here and be sensible, I get to go with you and be stupid. Damon's already got me a ticket. You can thank him later.'

'Thanking him isn't exactly what I have in mind.'

'Damon cares for you, Lena. He already has one sibling missing. He doesn't want another gone and I don't want to have to explain to Jared why the hell I let you go looking for him alone. It'll be bad enough trying to explain why I let you look for him at all.'

'You approve of what he's doing,' she said sourly. 'You don't want him safe. You want him to find out who sabotaged the East Timor run.'

'Damn right I do.'

'What'd you and Jared do? Toss a coin to see who went and who stayed to look after the invalid?'

'Didn't have to. He went. I stayed.' Trig eyed her flatly and Lena was the first to look away. She hadn't been the best of company these past nineteen months—too jacked up on painkillers and self-pity to take it easy on anyone. Too focused on getting through the day upright to worry about hurting anyone else's feelings along the way. Trig deserved better from her. Her family deserved better from her.

'Sorry,' she said and got a knee nudge from those long lanky legs in reply. 'I am sorry.'

'I know.'

But unless she actually *did* something about changing her mindset and her ways, sorry was just another empty word.

'You sitting next to me on this flight?' she asked.

Trig nodded, his eyes scanning the other passengers.

'Don't suppose Damon upgraded us to Business while he was deep in the bowels of the airline's supposedly secure system?'

'He did. Said we'd need the leg room. You need to check in with the boarding staff.'

Call it fate, intervention or the joys of having a computer-hacking genius for a brother, but the overhead speaker system chose that moment to request her presence at the boarding desk.

'You want me to get that?' Trig asked.

'No.' Lena made it to her feet. 'I can do it.'

It was to Trig's credit that he merely watched as she walked carefully to the service desk and exchanged her economy ticket for a business class one.

No credit to him at all when he sauntered over, face tight as he wrapped one arm around her waist and another beneath her knees and carried her silently back to her seat.

She wasn't grateful for his silence or his strength.

She wasn't.

They'd travelled together before. Eaten together, slept beside each other on beaches and in ditches. Lena knew Trig's scent, the long lines of his back and the breadth of his shoulders. Shoulders built to cry on, though she rarely had. Strength enough to carry others, though he'd never had to carry her.

Until she'd been shot.

A part of her hated that she couldn't match him any more. Couldn't pit her speed and agility against his brute force and make a proper competition out of it. The rest of her just wanted to curl up against his strength and take shelter from the pain.

The boarding call for their flight came over the speaker system.

'Lena—' began Trig, and she knew what he was going to say before he said it. She stopped him because she didn't want to hear yet another round of how she was too frail for this and how she should leave well enough alone.

'Don't tell me to reconsider,' she said and knew the threadiness of her voice for desperation. 'Please. I have to find him. I have to see for myself that he's okay. As soon as I know that, I'll leave. I promise. But I have to know that he's okay. I need him to see that *I'm* okay.'

Trig said nothing, just reached for Lena's little travel backpack sitting on the seat beside her. Reached for it at the same time she did.

'I can—' she began.

'Lena, if you don't let me carry your bag, I'm probably going to shoot you myself,' he said with exaggerated mildness. 'I want to help. You might even say I *need* to help...same way you need to see your brother and fix things with him. So let go of the *goddamn bag*.'

She let go of the bag. Trig didn't really have a hair trigger. Not all of the time.

'I don't think you'd shoot me,' she murmured finally. 'Even if you did have your gun. I think you're all bluff.'

'Am not.' Trig fell into step beside her—no small feat for a man whose stride was a good foot longer than hers. 'I'm ruthless and menacing and perfectly capable of following through on my threats. I wish you'd remember that.'

Maybe if she didn't know him so well, she'd think him more menacing. Trouble was she knew how gentle those big hands could be when it came to wounded things. Knew that he'd cut his hands off before hurting her.

Enough with the fixation on his hands.

They boarded the plane and found their seats. Trig stowed their bags and watched her settle tentatively into the wide and comfy seat. Ten seconds later he dangled a little pillow in front of her nose. Lena took it and set it at the small of her back.

Better.

'You got a plan for when we get to Istanbul?' Trig gave her another pillow and she contemplated swatting him with it, but tucked it down the side of the seat instead. She could always smother him with it later.

'I have a plan,' she said. 'And a meeting with Amos Carter in two days' time.'

'Please tell me you're not basing this entire journey

on Carter being able to tell you where Jared is,' said Trig. 'Because I've already shaken that tree. He *thought* he saw him in Bodrum but he didn't get close enough for a positive ID. That was six weeks ago.'

'I know that. And if Amos has nothing more to add I'm heading for Bodrum to play tourist and see what I can see. My eyes are better than his. I know Jared's habits. If he's there I'll find him. If he's been there, I'll find out where he's gone.'

She eyed Trig speculatively, trying to figure the best way to fit him into her plan. 'We could pretend to be holidaying together. We could be on our honeymoon. Good cover.'

Trig looked startled. And then he looked wary. 'Not necessarily. Bodrum's a tourist mecca. Boats. Parties. Outdoor nightclubs. Vice. We're probably going to be exploring that vice. I don't think pretending to be married would help at all.'

'You're absolutely right,' said Lena, perfectly willing to improve on her current plan. 'I could be your pimp instead. You could be Igor The Masterful. There could be leather involved.'

'Yeah, let's not go there either.'

Lena smiled at the flight hostess standing right behind him. To the hostie's credit she didn't bat an eyelash at the wayward conversation, just took her tongs and handed Trig a steaming flannel. She handed one to Lena too. Lena thanked her sweetly and shook it out and wiped hands and arms all the way to the elbows.

Trig sat down and draped his over his face.

'I'm still here,' said Lena.

'Don't remind me.'

'At least it's not the belly of a Hercules,' she said. 'And your legs actually fit in the space they've been given. It's all win.'

'I'm over winning.' She could still make out the words, muffled as they were beneath the face cloth. 'These days I'm all about risk analysis and minimising collateral damage.'

Well, hell. 'When did you grow up?'

'Twenty-second of April, twenty eleven.'

The day she'd been shot.

TWO

——

Twenty-six hours later Trig collected their bags and herded Lena out of Ataturk airport space and into a rusty, pale blue taxi. No fuss, no big deal made about Lena's slow and steady walking pace, and she was grateful for that. Grateful too that Trig had chosen to accompany her.

'Where to?' asked the driver in perfectly serviceable English as he opened the boot and swung their luggage into it, smoothly cataloguing them as foreigners and English-speaking ones at that. The street kids here could do much the same. Pick a German out of a crowd. An American. The English. Apparently it had something to do with shoes.

'The Best Southern Presidential Hotel near the Grand Bazaar,' Lena told the driver. 'And can you do something else for us? Can you take us past the Blue Mosque on the way there?'

'Madam, it would be my uttermost pleasure to do that for you,' announced the beaming driver. 'This is your first visit to our magnificent city, no? You and your husband must also journey to Topkapi Sarayi and Ayasofya. And the Bazaar of course. My cousin sells silk carpets there. I shall inform him of your imminent arrival and he shall treat you like family. Here.' The driver turned towards them, waving a small cardboard square. 'My cousin's business card. His shop is situated along Sahaflar Caddesi. It is a street of many sharks. *Many* sharks, but not my cousin. Tell him Yasar Sahin sent you. This is me. I have written it on the card for you already.'

Trig took the card from the driver in silence, probably in the hope that the driver would turn around and drive. Lena grinned. Trig had a weakness for carpets and rugs and wall hangings and tapestries. She had no idea why.

'You know you want one,' she murmured.

'Don't you dare mention jewellery,' he murmured back, but Yasar Sahin heard him.

'Are you looking for gold?' Another card appeared in the driver's nimble fingers. 'Silver? This man is my *brother* and his jewellery will make your wife weep.'

'I don't want her to weep,' said Trig but he took that card too. He didn't mention that Lena wasn't his wife.

'Are you hungry?' asked the driver. 'On this road is my favourite kebab stand. Best in the city.'

'Another brother?' asked Lena.

'Twin,' said the driver and Lena laughed.

They didn't get the kebabs, they saw the Blue

Mosque at dusk and they arrived at the hotel without mishap.

Trig tipped well because Lena was still smiling. He got Yasar's personal business card for his trouble. 'Because I am also a tour guide and fixer,' said Yasar.

'Fixer?'

'Problem solver.'

Of course he was.

The hotel Lena had chosen to stay in was mid-range and well located. She'd told the check-in clerk that Trig was her husband, who'd joined her on the trip unexpectedly, and the clerk had added Trig's details to the booking without so much as a murmur.

'You sure about this?' he murmured as the clerk went to fetch their door cards.

'Why? You want another room?'

He didn't know.

'It's a twin room. Two beds.'

Still one room though.

And boy were quarters snug.

Trig eyed the short distance between the two beds with misgivings. They'd weathered plenty, he and Lena. Sharing a hotel room was not on the list.

He put her bag on the rack at the end of the bed farthest away from the door. Lena inspected the bathroom and proclaimed it satisfactory, because she'd wanted one with a spa bath and got it. Next thing he knew, the bath taps were on and Lena was rummaging through her belongings for fresh clothes.

'You want to shower while the bath is running?'

she asked him. 'Because—fair warning—when I get in the bath I am not going to want to get out.'

'You're sore?'

'I just want to work the kinks out.'

'Right.' Trig cleared his throat and opened his bag, staring down at the mess of clothes he hadn't bothered to fold, and tried not to think about Lena, naked in a bath not ten feet away from him. 'So...okay, yeah. I can shower now.' He grabbed at a faded pair of jeans and an equally well-worn T-shirt and then paused. 'Where do you want to go for dinner?' This could, conceivably, affect his choice of T-shirt.

'I'm all in favour of room service, provided the menu looks good. And it's not because I don't want to walk anywhere,' she added defensively. 'Room service for dinner this evening has always been part of the plan.'

Far be it from him to mess with the plan. He eyeballed the distance between the beds again. 'Is it just me or is this room kind of small?'

'Maybe if you'd stop *growing*...'

'I have.' Okay, so he was extra tall and his shoulders were broad. For the most part, he was good with it. 'You just think I should have stopped *sooner*.' He eyed his little double bed with misgivings. 'That's not a double bed. It's a miniature double bed.'

'Princess.'

'Are we bickering?' he asked. 'Because Poppy tells me she's heartily sick of our bickering. I thought I might give it up for Lent.'

'It's not Lent,' Lena informed him. 'Besides, I like bickering with you. Makes me feel all comfortable and peachy-normal.'

Trig snorted. At sixteen, bickering with Lena had been his first line of defence against anyone discovering just how infatuated he was with her. He was still gone on her, no question. But these days the bickering got old fast.

He found his toiletries bag and stalked into the bathroom, only to find that that room was the size of a bath *mat* and that the spa was filling ever so slowly— a sneaky deterrent to filling it at all. Instead of four walls, the bathroom had two walls, a side door and one of those shuttered, half-walls dividing it from the main room. Trig reached for the shutters.

She-who-bickered would of a certainty want them shut.

He eyed the bathroom door and the floor mat in its way. He could shut that at the last minute. Never let it be said that Adrian Sinclair had more than a regular dislike for small spaces. Just don't ever put him in a submarine.

'Hey, Trig.' Lena's voice floated through the door. 'Five things you never wanted to be. And don't say, "Your babysitter".'

Never wanted to be in love with my best friend's sister, he thought darkly. Especially since she'd never once given him the slightest encouragement.

'I never wanted to be a motor mechanic,' he said instead.

'Be serious.'

'I am serious.' He turned on the shower taps, hoping for a little pressure. Nope. Maybe if he turned the bath taps off. He shucked his clothes and dropped them on the floor. And Lena appeared in the doorway.

'Dammit, Lena! Close quarters!' But he didn't reach for a towel or turn to hide his body. Most of it she'd seen before, and as for the rest...well...nothing to be ashamed of there.

Lena dropped her gaze, but not to the floor. She swallowed hard. 'I, ah—'

'Yes?' he enquired silkily, half of him annoyed and half most emphatically not.

His brain thought she was objectifying him and he objected to that.

His body didn't give a damn whether she objectified him or not.

'I, ah—' Finally she dragged her gaze up and over the rest of him and then, with what seemed like a whole lot of effort, looked away. 'Sorry. Pretty sure I'll remember what I wanted to tell you sooner or later.'

'Size queen,' he challenged softly.

'Yeah, well. Who knew?' She did the quickest about-turn he'd seen from her in a long time and headed back into the other part of the room, the part he couldn't see. 'I mean, I'd heard rumours... Your old girlfriends aren't exactly discreet.'

'No?' He'd had girlfriends over the years—not plenty, but enough. He'd tried hard to fall for each and every one. 'What are they?'

'Grateful,' she said dryly. 'Now I know why.'

'You really don't,' he felt obliged to point out, and left the bathroom door open and turned back towards the shower. 'Who's to say it wasn't my winning personality?'

'You do like to win,' she said as he stepped beneath the spray and closed the shower door. Surely one closed door between them would be enough.

'You keep saying that.'

'Only because it's true.'

All throughout their teens and beyond, he, Lena and Jared had pushed each other to be faster, cannier, more fearless. It had got them into plenty of trouble. Got them into the Secret Intelligence Service too. Jared rising through the ranks because he was a leader born, Trig and Lena rising with him because they had skills too and the suits knew the makings of a crack infiltration team when they saw one.

No space between him and Lena at all when it came to what they knew about each other. No strength or flaw left unexamined. No shortage of loyalty or love. Lena loved him like a brother and like a comrade-in-arms, and that was worth something. It was.

But sometimes she saw the reckless boy he'd once been rather than the man he was now.

Sometimes she coaxed him into competitive games he no longer had the heart to play.

He raised his voice so that she'd hear him over the spray. 'Is there a burger on that menu?'

'Hang on...' She came back to the bathroom doorway, casual as you please now that a plate of frosted glass stood between her and his nakedness. 'Yes, there's a burger on the menu. Lamb burger on Turkish. Surprise. There's also meatballs and potatoes, salads, green beans, and lots of pastries.'

'Baklava?'

'Oodles of baklava. Walnut, pistachio, cashew, pine nuts... You want yours drizzled in rose water?'

'Rather have it in my mouth.' He squirted shampoo in his palm and raised his hands to his head.

'Are you posing on purpose?'

'Are you looking on purpose?' It seemed like a reasonable reply. 'Because I've no objection. You want a closer look, all you gotta do is say.' He reached for the shower door and smirked as Lena squeaked a protest and fled. 'Thought you were fearless.'

'That was before I got scarred for life. Now I'm wary. Don't want to get scarred for life twice.'

'Amen to that,' he muttered, all playfulness gone as he shoved his head beneath the spray again, the better to chase away the image of Lena on her back in the mud, her guts hot and slippery against his hands while the world around them exploded. Scrub that memory from his mind.

Good if he could.

'What kind of baklava did you want?' asked Lena.

'Is there a mixed plate?'

'I can ask.'

He heard Lena ordering the food.

He tried to think about the real reason they were

in Turkey. Get Lena's eyes on Jared and Jared's on her. Let them realise that everyone was okay and then get Lena the hell out of harm's way before Jared could tear him a new one.

Simple plan.

Didn't take a genius to know that the execution was going to be a bitch.

Trig emerged from the bathroom squeaky clean and somewhat calmer about sharing a hotel room with Lena. Lena had the television on and was standing to one side of it, flicking through the channels. She glanced at him, eyes wary. He thought she had relaxed a bit. Possibly because he had his clothes on.

'Food'll be here in an hour,' she said. 'I thought you'd take longer. I thought I might soak in the spa.'

Soak. Right. Lena was about to get naked and soapy not five steps from where he was standing, and he was going to ignore her and not even think about palming the bulge in his pants, not even just to rearrange it.

'I need a walk,' he muttered. And tried not to slam the door on his way out.

Lena sagged against the nearest wall the minute the door closed behind him. She didn't know what to make of Trig's moods these days—one minute teasing, short-tempered the next. That was *her* bailiwick, not Trig's. Trig was the even-tempered one, rock-steady in any crisis.

Calm, even when she'd been flat on her back in the

sticky grey clay of East Timor and he'd been holding her guts in place with his hands. Calm when Jared had skidded in beside him and told him to get out of the way and Trig had said no, just no, but Jared had backed off, and gone and stolen transport and got them to safety while Trig kept Lena alive.

Trig, steady as you please, as the world around her had turned cold and grey.

'Don't you,' he'd said, his voice hard and implacable in her ear. '*Fight*, damn you. You always do.'

She'd fought.

She was still fighting.

Her injuries. Her reliance on others.

Her feelings for Trig and the memory of his cheek against hers and the gutted murmur of his voice when he'd thought her unconscious.

'Stay with me, Lena. Don't you *dare* go where I can't follow.'

Closest he'd ever come to saying he had feelings for her that weren't exactly brotherly.

Once upon a time, maybe, yeah, she'd have been all over that. All over *him* if he'd given her enough encouragement.

But now?

No way.

Because what could she offer him now? She who could barely hold herself together from one day to the next. She whose default setting ran more towards lashing out at people than to loving them.

And then there was the matter of her not so minor

physical injuries. A body as beautiful as Trig's deserved a beautiful body beneath it, not one like hers, all scarred and barely working. No babies from this body, and Trig knew it. He'd been there when the doctor had broken *that* news, only it was hardly news to Lena because given the mess her body had been in at the time she'd already figured as much.

It had been news to Trig though, and she'd plucked at a thread in the loose-woven hospital blanket and watched beneath lowered lashes as he'd dropped his head to the web of his hands and kept it there for the duration of the doctor's explanation. No comment from him at all when he'd finally lifted his head, just a stark, shattered glance in her direction before he'd swiftly looked away.

Not pity. He didn't do pity.

It had looked a lot like grief.

A bottle of red wine stood on the counter above the little hotel-room fridge. Lena cracked it and poured herself a generous glass full. She picked through her suitcase for a change of clothes and took those and the wine with her to the bathroom.

Water would help. Water always helped her relax and think clearly.

Find Jared. That was her goal.

Keep Lena out of trouble. She was pretty sure that was Trig's goal.

And then, once the world was set right, she and Trig could find a new way of communicating. One that didn't involve him being overprotective and her being defensive. One that involved more honesty and less bickering. Lena sipped at her wine and stared pensively at the slowly filling tub.

One that involved a little more wholly platonic appreciation for the person he was.

THREE

Trig returned just as their dinner arrived. He gave her a nod, tipped the man for his service and started moving dishes from the room-service cart to the little table for two over by the window.

Lena poured him a wine and another one for herself. She didn't ask him about his walk straight away. Given the tension that had followed him into the room, she figured she might hold that totally innocuous question in reserve.

'You taken any painkillers?' he asked, not an unreasonable question given how much of the wine she'd drunk. What could she say? It had been a long bath.

'Not yet. Tonight I'm rocking the red wine instead.'

'Any particular reason why?'

'Long day.' You. 'New city.' You. Never want to be on the wrong side of you.

She used to be able to read him just by looking at him. These days she'd have better luck reading Farsi.

Trig took a seat, lifted his burger and bit into it, chewing steadily.

Lena sat opposite, picked at her spicy chicken salad and drank some more wine.

'When are you meeting with Carter?'

'Tomorrow at two p.m. at the Nuruosmaniye Gate of the Grand Bazaar. You want to come?'

'I'll watch.'

'From afar?'

'Not that far.'

'Play your cards right and I might even buy you a silk scarf.'

Trig smiled. 'Not my thing.'

'How's the burger?'

Trig nodded and took another hefty bite.

The burger was fine.

He looked at her salad and kept on chewing, right up until he swallowed. 'Get your own,' he said darkly.

Mind reader. 'I'll have you know that this salad's delicious. Crisp little salad leaves and cucumber. Tasty tomato. All very healthy.' How was she to know that she'd take one look at Trig's burger and want something drippy too.

Trig's sigh was well practised as he broke what was left of his burger in two and held out one half to her.

She took it with a grin. 'My brothers aren't nearly such soft touches.'

'I'm not one of your brothers,' he said, and something about the way he said it shut her up completely.

Good thing she had the burger to concentrate on.

And the wine. And those two little double beds that hovered in her view no matter where she looked.

'Adrian, is there a problem? Between you and me?' She hurried on, never mind his frown. 'Because we've been friends a long time and I know I've relied on you far more than I should these past couple of years. You've been more than patient with me, and I'm grateful, because I know damn well that I don't deserve anyone's patience a lot of the time. It's just…lately I get the feeling that you've had enough of me. And that would be perfectly understandable. *Is* perfectly understandable. And if that's the case, you need to stand back and let me take care of myself. I can, you know.'

'You sure about that?'

'Sure as I can be without actually having done it. I have this family who seem to think I'm fragile, you see. They baby me. They send you to handle me when they can't. I don't think that's fair on you. You don't have to do that. You have your own life to live.'

He thought on that, right through what was left of his burger, and then he drained his wine and turned his attention to the baklava.

'Tell me why I'm here,' he said finally.

That was easy. 'You're the family-appointed babysitter, sent to keep me out of trouble.'

'That's one reason. But it's not the main one.'

'Loyalty to Jared.'

'Has nothing to do with it.'

'You have a hankering for baklava?'

'Not enough to travel halfway round the world for

it.' Trig eyed her steadily and no matter how much Lena ached to look away, she couldn't. She couldn't find her breath either.

'You're well enough to go chasing after Jared,' he said finally. 'I figure you're well enough to hear me out. Not going to jump you, Lena. Nothing you don't want. But you need to know that I'm here because I want to be here. With you. Because there's pretty much nowhere else I'd rather be than with you. You need to know that I have feelings for you that are in no way brotherly. You need to know that I both love and hate it when you treat me like family.'

He took a deep breath. 'You also need to know what you do to me when you book us into a hotel as husband and wife. Because it gives me ideas.'

She didn't understand. He'd peppered her with too much information and not enough time to process any of it. 'I— Pardon?'

'I want you.'

'You—do?'

He looked at her as if she were a little bit dim. 'Yes.'

'But...you can't.'

'Pretty sure I can.'

'I'm broken.'

'Nah, just banged up.'

'I'm *me*.'

'Yes.' He was looking at her as if she were minus a few brain cells again. He was just so...calm.

And she wasn't. Somehow she had to bring this

farce of a conversation under control. 'How's the bak-lava?'

'Tastes like dust.'

'More wine?' She poured him some anyway, whether he wanted it or not, and maybe that wasn't such a good idea because he drained it in one long swallow. 'You need to give me some time with this.'

'Little hint for you, Lena: this doesn't require much thinking. We've known each other a long time. I've been trying to impress you since primary school. You're either impressed or you're not. You either want me or you don't.'

'It's not that simple.'

'Yeah, it is.'

'I saw your body earlier.' She didn't know how to say what she wanted to say. 'It's perfect.'

'It's skin.'

'It's still perfect.'

'Still just skin. You think I can't see beneath yours?' He eyed her steadily. 'You have flaws. So do I. No one's going into this blind.'

'Look at me, Adrian. Think of all the things you can do that I can't do any more. I'd hold you back and you'd come to hate me for it. *I'd* come to hate me for it. You'd have to be blind to want this.'

'I'm not blind,' he said grimly. 'This *can* work—you and me. You just have to want it to.' He sat back in his chair and pushed a hand through his dark shaggy curls. 'This isn't going well, is it? You don't think of me in that way at all.'

'I didn't say that! Don't put words in my mouth. God.' Trust her to push him away when she didn't mean to. She just didn't know how to *not* push him away now that he wanted to get closer. 'You're important to me, Adrian. You occupy a huge part of my life and always have done. Aren't you scared that if this doesn't work out, we'll lose everything else we *do* have?'

'Scared is watching you slide into unconsciousness for the sixth time in as many hours. Scared is thinking you're going to die in my arms. This doesn't even rate a mention on the fear scale.'

'Speak for yourself. I'm terrified here.' Lena reached over and circled his wrist with her fingers as best she could, one fingertip to his pulse point and her heart beating a rapid tattoo. His pulse skittered all over the place too. 'You're not that calm.'

'Could be I'm a *little* nervous. Doesn't mean I haven't thought it through,' he said stubbornly. He withdrew his hand from beneath her fingers and headed for the bedside phone. He picked it up, pressed a button and waited.

'What are you doing?'

'You said you needed some time with this. I'm giving you some.' He turned his head into the phone a little. 'This is Adrian Sinclair. I'm going to need a second room. King bed this time.' He listened a moment. 'No, it doesn't have to be connected to this one.' He waited another moment. 'Thanks.'

He put the phone down. 'A porter will be here for my bag in a few minutes.'

'You didn't have to do that.'

He didn't have to repack his bag. His stuff was good to go. She didn't want him to go. 'Adrian, I—'

'See you for breakfast, yeah?'

Hell. 'Yeah.' She tried again. 'It wasn't a no. I haven't said no to anything you've put forward. I *have* thought of you like that. From time to time. I'm female. You're you. Who wouldn't?'

She thought she saw a glimmer of a smile.

'But think about it, Adrian. Are you sure this is what you want? Because I really don't think you *have* thought this through.'

He frowned down at her, and then he leaned down and gently brushed his lips against the corner of her mouth. His lips were soft and warm. Lena felt her eyes flutter closed.

He drew back slowly and she wondered when his eyes had got so dark and hungry.

'I've thought it through. You need to do the same.'

He picked up his bag; he walked to the door.

And it clicked shut behind him.

As far as declarations of intent were concerned, that one could have gone better, decided Trig as he headed for the lifts. Lena had never handled romance well. In her teens she'd been too forward with boys, too fearless, too competitive, and she'd sent them running. Later on she'd got the hang of not scaring away potential suitors—she'd even taken a few of them to her bed, but for some reason known only to her none of them had ever measured up. Not in her eyes.

Not in Trig's or Jared's eyes either.

So she'd had standards that had suited them all.

Standards based around her father, the highly successful international banker. Around Damon, adrenaline junkie and hacker extraordinaire. Around Jared, who feared nothing and regularly achieved the impossible.

Standards that made her picky, and then, when she did break things off with the latest but not quite greatest, she'd start second-guessing herself and getting all despondent because the jerk she'd just let go had told her she wasn't feminine enough or that she needed to soften up a bit before any man would take her seriously. Sour grapes, a parting shot, but Lena had never seen it that way.

She'd mope for a few days and then Jared would tell her he was going skydiving on Friday and that he'd saved her a chute.

She'd try and be softer with other people for a bit and then Trig would turn up with his lightest kiteboarding rig, and there'd be a thirty-knot cross-shore wind blowing and he'd eyeball the conditions and they'd barely be manageable and he'd ask if she wanted to go break something.

The answer to that being, *'Hell, yes.'* Always yes.

Until she'd got shot and everything had changed for all of them.

These days no one challenged Lena to push harder or go faster, even though she still pushed herself.

These days he looked at her with concern in his eyes; he knew he did. And she looked at him and told him to go away.

Rough couple of years.

But things were getting better now. Lena was getting better now and together they could find a new way of doing things and of being with each other if only she'd try.

The lift doors opened. A uniformed boy gave him an appraising stare. 'Mr Sinclair?'

Trig nodded.

'Let me take your luggage.' If the boy wondered why Mr Sinclair needed to change rooms, he was too discreet to ask. 'Room 406 for you, Mr Sinclair. I have your entry cards here.'

Trig stepped into the lift.

He just had to convince her to try.

FOUR

—

Trig woke to the sound of morning prayer at a nearby mosque. His bed had been big enough but his dreams had been chaotic. Loss, always loss. Lena walking away from him because he'd asked too much of her. Lena disappearing into the gluggy grey mud of East Timor. Slipping away from him, one way or another, with Trig powerless to prevent any of it.

The prayer song was hypnotic.

Trig closed his eyes and ran his hands through his hair and sent up a prayer of his own that this day would be a good day and that Lena wouldn't be freaking out about last night's declaration of undying devotion—or whatever it was that he'd declared.

She wouldn't run; she was smarter than that.

But she might feel uneasy with him and he wouldn't put it past her to have argued herself around to thinking that she wasn't good enough for him or that he'd be better off without her. For someone so magnificent, she had the lowest sense of self-worth he'd ever encountered.

She'd told him once that it came of being an ordinary person in an extraordinary family. She'd never seen herself as extraordinary too.

He reached for the hotel phone, tapped in the other room number and waited.

She wouldn't have done a runner. If nothing else, she knew he'd track her through Amos Carter if he had to. She might reschedule but she wouldn't blow that meeting off. Her need to find Jared was too strong.

'What?' she finally mumbled, once she'd picked up.

'You want to have breakfast at this little café I saw on my walk last night?'

'When?'

'Now.'

'What time is it?'

'Five-seventeen.'

Lena groaned, a sleepy, sexy sound that had him shifting restlessly. 'You want to have breakfast *now*?'

'I'm starving.'

'You're always starving.'

'Their breakfast special is lentil soup, a loaf of sourdough and a big chunk of cheese.'

'Go get 'em, Tiger. Bring me back a cup of tea,' she muttered and hung up.

Trig grinned and shoved the sheet aside, suddenly hungry to seize the day. She hadn't said no and she hadn't been wary. She hadn't said, 'Darling, come make me yours,' yet either, but that was pure fantasy anyway.

He got breakfast.

He went walking and found the gate where Lena would meet up with Carter and set about exploring exit options and observation points. By the time the seven a.m. prayer session sounded, he was back at the hotel and knocking on Lena's door, takeaway tea in one hand and a tub of yoghurt and honey in the other.

'Breakfast,' he said when she opened the door, and she let him through and closed the door behind him and yawned.

She looked like a waif. A little too slender, a halo of tangled black hair and those startling bluish-grey eyes, smudged with black lashes. A modelling agency had offered to contract her once after seeing her on the beach. Surfing sponsors had come after her too. She'd turned down both offers with startled surprise. Couldn't see what they'd seen in her. Didn't want what they'd offered anyway.

'Is this the courting you?' she wanted to know as he set the tea and yoghurt on the table.

'This is the impatient me,' he said. 'You've seen this me before. I'm waiting to see if you want me to court you before I start that.'

'My mistake.' Lena smirked and carefully removed the lid on her tea. 'What's got you all pepped up?'

'You mean besides wanting to know if you'll go out with me?'

'Yeah, besides that. Because I'm not awake enough

yet to make a definitive decision on that. I couldn't think clearly enough to make a decision on it last night either.'

'Red wine does that.'

'True.' She sipped at her tea and let out an appreciative sigh. 'So you're happy this morning because...'

'You have got to see this bazaar.'

'You're excited about *shopping*?'

'It's not shopping, it's haggling. It's a blood sport.'

'Is anything even open yet?'

'Couple of stalls are.'

'What did you buy?'

'Carpet. But I haven't bought it yet. I've just had it set aside so I can think about it.'

'Uh-huh. How much?'

'That's what we're negotiating.'

'Ballpark.'

'It's a really nice carpet. Silk.'

'Uh-huh.'

Seven thousand dollars *was* a lot to pay for a two metre by one point six metre bit of mat that people walked on. 'It's an investment piece.'

'Is it magic?'

'I didn't ask. Maybe you should come with me when I go back.'

'When are you going back?'

'After I've shopped around.'

'Who are you and what have you done with Trig?'

'Could be I'm nesting,' he said. Way to harp on a tricky subject. 'You all the way awake yet?'

'No.'

'Because if you are, now would be a good time to tell me if you're going to go out with me.'

'Still weighing the pros and cons.'

There was just no rushing her these days. 'I brought you breakfast. That would be a pro.'

'You also woke me up at five a.m.'

'You're welcome.'

He could make her snort. That had to count for something.

'How's the body this morning?'

'Functional,' she said around a mouthful of yoghurt. 'Stop fussing. Boyfriends don't fuss.'

'Now you're just making shit up.'

'No, I'm pretty sure it's true.'

He shook his head, slid her a sideways glance. 'Pursuit aside, how are we tracking with regards to our regular relationship? The one that *doesn't* have me in knots. We good?'

'Yeah.' She sounded a little uncertain. 'We're good.'

They made it through the morning, mostly because Trig headed back out again to look at carpets, and then it was time to meet Carter, with Lena taking point and Trig bleeding into the bustle at the gate. Another tourist, one of many, and maybe he was meeting someone or perhaps he was just taking a breather before diving into the next shop full of goodies. Either way, nothing untoward here.

He spotted Carter moments before the older man

made him, but they didn't acknowledge each other. He and Carter had worked together before, albeit briefly, back in the days when Carter had worked for ASIS. Carter would know Trig was running surveillance on the meet. Carter probably had someone else doing the same.

Carter approached Lena and held out his hands and she took them and smiled as he kissed her on each cheek. Old acquaintances and all for show. Trig ground his teeth and watched some more as Carter and Lena strolled through the gate and into the bazaar, their pace leisurely and their conversation animated.

Trig made a process out of checking his phone as he waited to see who else might be headed that way before he too took a stroll. It was a busy gate. A lot of people followed Carter and Lena into the bazaar.

He kept them in sight while he browsed and they browsed and then five minutes later Carter bought Lena a scoop full of candied citrus, presented it to her with a smile, kissed her once again on each cheek and, between one blink and the next, disappeared into the ether.

Lena didn't look back at Trig; she knew this game too well for that. She bought three silk scarves and a handful of sugared almonds. She paused outside a shop filled with carpets and the vendor—and probably his brother—instantly tried to woo her in. She offered them almonds, which they refused. They offered her apple tea, and carpet viewing, which she refused. With a great deal of hand waving all round, everyone called it quits and Lena moved on.

No one but Trig followed her, and no one followed him, but he stayed on her tail just that little bit longer because they didn't know what Jared was into and because Carter was just that little bit unpredictable when it came to who he was working for at any one time.

Lena turned down a side lane of the bazaar, and then another. They'd reached a narrow walkway full of fabrics—an explosion of colour pinned to walls and strung across ceilings. Fabric everywhere and a group of youths with fierce eagle eyes coming towards them. They passed Lena, jostled her, and no one reached out to break her fall as she went down hard. She hit her head on the metal foot of a display rack. She didn't get up.

By the time Trig reached her, her wallet was gone and so were the youths. A few people yelled out. No one gave chase.

'Lena.' She looked so very small and crumpled. She wasn't conscious and he didn't want to move her. He reached for the pulse point at her wrist. *'Lena.'*

Other people had crouched down beside them. 'She's with you?' one man asked and Trig nodded. Hands reached out to gently shake her. He didn't know who they belonged to.

Don't,' he growled and pushed all those other hands away, dog with a bone and he didn't care who knew it. 'Don't touch her.'

Someone else tried to get the crowd around them to move back a step. Someone passed a cloth through to the man who'd spoken earlier and he handed it to Trig. 'For her head,' the man said and used gestures to suggest that Trig wipe her face.

The cloth was wet and smelled only of water. Trig drew it across Lena's forehead.

She didn't even flinch.

Trig looked for a bump on Lena's skull and found it towards the back of her head. Not that big, according to his fingers, but big enough to knock her unconscious nonetheless. 'Can you call me an ambulance?' he asked the man.

'Private or public?'

'Private.'

'Take taxi—is faster,' said a woman, but the man held up his finger and shook his head, and then started arguing with the woman, too fast for Trig to even try to understand. They weren't a threat. They were trying to help. He thought the man might be the proprietor of the nearby stall.

Lena stirred and Trig wiped the cloth across her forehead again. Her eyelashes fluttered.

'Lena?'

But she didn't come round fully.

Another person handed him an unopened bottle of water. 'Thank you,' he said as the crowd around them grew larger and talk turned to the pickpocket gangs and notifying the police that they were back in the area. Lena opened her eyes again and this time they stayed open while Trig checked her pupils for unevenness and then covered her eyes with his palm.

'Try and keep your eyes open and in a few more seconds I'll take my hand away,' he told her quietly, while his heart thundered and his mind flashed back to the ambush in East Timor. Some injuries were messy. This one was not. Didn't mean the outcome couldn't be catastrophic. 'I'm going to check your pupils for responsiveness to light.'

'You're a doctor?' asked Trig's new best friend, the one who'd called for an ambulance.

'Medic.' He had some combat first-aid training, that was all. 'Not a doctor.' Please don't let her pupils be blown.

He took his hand away from Lena's eyes and her pupils responded. Lena looked bewildered. Her eyes searched the crowd and finally came to rest back on him.

'Where am I?' she asked.

'The Grand Bazaar.' And when that didn't seem to ring any bells, 'Istanbul.'

'Oh.'

'You fell and hit your head. Pickpockets. They got your wallet.'

'Gonna be sick,' she said and rolled onto her side, but she wasn't sick, she just closed her eyes and put her cheek to the floor and slipped into a state of not-quite-thereness.

He tried not to let that worry him as he held the

wet flannel to the bump on her head, and damn but it felt bigger.

She opened her eyes again a few minutes later. 'Just rest,' he told her. 'Don't need to move you yet. An ambulance is on its way.'

'Here's hoping I have insurance,' she murmured, and fixed him with a dazed gaze.

''Course you do.'

'Next question—'

He had to lean down to even hear her.

'—Who are you?'

She didn't like hospitals. She could barely remember her own name, but she knew with utter certainty that she did *not* like hospitals. And that she'd been in them a lot. Her body confirmed it when they sent her for the MRI and asked her to change into a gown. The scars on her lower belly and high on her leg told of a major collision between her body and...something. Car crash, maybe.

She couldn't quite remember.

'You have titanium pins and plates in your left leg and hip,' the big guy had said when he'd helped her fill out a medical history form, finally taking the clipboard and pen from her and filling out the information sheet himself. 'You've had several recent operations and intensive and ongoing physiotherapy.'

He knew her blood type and he knew her name.

Lena Sinclair.

She knew her name was Lena. Bits and pieces of

her memory were starting to come back. The scarves hanging in the marketplace. The impression that someone, or several someones, had been following her. Her name was Lena, Lena Sinclair, and the big guy, who she couldn't quite remember...

He was her husband.

His name was Adrian. She'd read it on his credit cards and on the hospital forms. Adrian Sinclair. Husband. And he seemed so familiar, hauntingly familiar, and he made her feel safe, and he'd hovered while the doctors had seen to her, and if she couldn't quite remember much about him at the moment, well, there were a lot of things she couldn't quite remember at the moment.

He was the most beautiful man she'd ever seen.

'My name's Lena, Lena Sinclair,' she told the doctors. 'I'm Australian and I was shopping in the Grand Bazaar when thieves knocked me to the ground and took off with my wallet.'

There'd been mutterings then, about the crime rate in the city. The police had been notified. Cards would be cancelled. Her husband would take care of it. 'Lena, relax,' he'd told her firmly. 'First things first. Just get the MRI done.'

Lena. Lena Sinclair.

She could remember pretty much everything that had happened since waking up in the bazaar. As for her life *before* then... She was Australian and she'd grown up on the beach with two brothers and a sister whose names she couldn't quite recall.

'Concussion,' the doctor told her. 'Minor head trauma.'

A cracking headache, nausea and, heavens, why did the lights have to be so bright?

'Temporary confusion and memory loss are both symptoms of concussion,' the doctor told her when Lena confessed to scrambled memories and a whole lot of fog. 'The painkillers I've given you won't have helped. You remember who you are?'

'Lena. Lena Sinclair.'

'You remember your family and your past?'

'Sort of.'

'It's common not to remember the events leading up to the knock on the head.'

Good to know she was common.

'Do you remember your husband?'

'Yes,' she said. She remembered that he made her feel safe. She remembered his hands.

'You need to rest your body and your brain,' the doctor told her. 'I've given you pain medication and something to minimise the swelling. I'm releasing you into the care of your husband, and if he hovers or wakes you several times through the night, it's because I've told him to. If you start to feel anxious, let him know. Should your headache or nausea worsen, should you become disoriented, should your co-ordination worsen...you let him know and he'll bring you back here.'

'Okay.'

'You already have co-ordination issues due to your

previous injuries. I'm not talking about those. I'm talking about new limitations, just so we're clear.'

'Clear,' she said faintly. She just wanted to get out of the hospital.

She hated hospitals.

And then they *were* out of the hospital and the street was unfamiliar and the smell of the city invaded her nostrils and she immediately wanted away from there too.

A taxi stood waiting for them. Her husband must have arranged it because the driver seemed to know him. 'Your lady wife *must* stay close to you,' he kept telling her stony-faced husband. 'It's not always safe here. Where did you and your lady wife *go?*'

'Just take us back to the hotel.' He could sound menacing when he wanted to, this husband she couldn't quite recall. He could make talkative taxi drivers shut the hell up and drive.

The hotel was a pleasant, mid-range affair, with a buffet restaurant that her husband glanced at as they headed across the foyer towards the lifts.

'Are you hungry?' she asked him.

'I could eat.'

He'd been at her side all day. In waiting rooms and examination rooms. He'd been her voice when she couldn't remember what she'd done to her leg. There'd been no time for him to slip out and grab some food.

'We could eat at the buffet,' she said, and made it sound like a question.

'I was thinking room service.'

Which could take some time to arrive. 'Or we could eat now.'

'You're hungry?'

'No, but you are. You fill up. I'll pick and choose. Everyone's a winner.'

'I'd rather get you back to the room.'

'The head is woolly but I'm feeling no pain,' she assured him. 'The painkillers are good and the food is right there. How about I let you know the minute I've had enough?'

He didn't look convinced.

'Okay, how about you watch me intently all through dinner and *you* let me know when I've had enough?'

'You look like you've had enough already.' Blunt, this husband of hers.

'I think I can stretch it another twenty minutes. Or we could stand here arguing.'

He smiled at that, really smiled, and Lena watched, mesmerised, for it was a wicked, charming smile full of warmth and wide approval.

'It is you,' he murmured, and steered her towards the restaurant entrance. He gave the maître d' their room number and saw her seated, but he didn't sit.

'I'm going to go change our booking. Get us another couple of days here. You be okay here while I do that?'

'I'll be fine.'

She watched him go. Broad shoulders, slim hips, long legs and all gorgeous.

And then he disappeared from sight and it took all her effort to quell the panic that arrived with his disappearance. *Breathe, Lena.* Everything was fine. She was fine.

They were staying here, they had a room here, and if she needed to get to it all she had to do was ask the front desk for a number and a key. Her memory would be back soon and her husband wasn't going anywhere. He'd be back soon too.

A waiter asked if she wanted anything to drink with dinner and she ordered fizzy water for them both. She had a feeling her husband drank beer, but she didn't know if he would want one with their meal. The waiter assured her that he would return once her husband did.

Five minutes later her husband returned.

'Done?' she queried.

'Done.'

'Where were we supposed to go after this?'

'You don't remember?'

'No.' No need to alarm him with how much she *didn't* remember. Yet. 'I'm a little fuzzy on the details.'

'We were going to Bodrum to find Jared.'

'Oh.' Was now a good time to tell him that she had no idea who Jared was? 'Right.'

Her husband, Adrian, was looking at her funny. And that name...her husband's name...didn't sit altogether right with her either. 'Do I call you something other than Adrian?'

'Trig,' he said gruffly. 'You call me Trig.'

'Okay.' She started to nod and then thought the better of it. 'Okay. Oh, and the waiter came by and I ordered you a soda water. I wasn't sure whether you'd want anything alcoholic.'

'Not tonight.' He followed her to the buffet. Stayed behind her while she browsed and added little spoonfuls of this and that to her plate. She waited for Trig to load up his plate, which he did—with generous helpings of pretty much everything.

Trig frowned at her half-filled plate.

'I'm probably going to have seconds,' she lied.

'You know I can tell when you're lying, right?'

She hadn't known that. She added a spoonful of what looked like sweet potato to her plate.

They returned to the table and sat. Trig ate, and Lena mostly watched. He took her close scrutiny in his stride.

'Why aren't we wearing our wedding rings?' she asked finally, and watched as her husband choked on his food.

He coughed, eyes watering, and reached for his water. 'What?' he croaked.

'At first I thought the thieves must have taken them too, but then I noticed that you're not wearing one either, and I'm pretty sure I gave you one.'

He blinked at that and took another great gulp of his water.

'Lena, exactly how much *do* you remember about your past?' Her husband's words came out measured and even but his gaze could probably have penetrated steel.

'Lots of bits and pieces,' she said. 'Lots. But I don't remember our wedding.'

'What's your maiden name?'

'Um—'

'Your brothers' names?'

'Dan. No, Damien.' One of them was called Damien.

'Damon.'

'Yes, Damon.' An image of a laughing, dark-haired boy on a surfboard came to her. 'He surfs. He loves the sea.' Trig remained stony-faced and Lena's confidence faltered. 'Doesn't he?'

'Yes.'

'See? Memory on the mend.'

But her husband didn't seem to think so. 'Lena, can you remember why we're even in Turkey?'

'Not really, no. Everything's foggy. But I do remember you. I know you. Feel safe with you. You're my husband.'

Trig.

A new and startling thought occurred to her—one that explained away her husband's grimness and their current lack of wedding rings. 'We're not *just*...just-married, are we? Were we going to buy rings here?' It made sense. It was almost coming back to her. 'Are we on our honeymoon?'

He didn't say anything for a very long time, and then he looked her dead in the eye and said, 'Yes.'

FIVE

——

She barely remembered him. Trig tried to conceal his growing panic beneath another mouthful of food. Lena really did think she was married to him. Because he'd told the hospital staff they were in order to get her the attention she'd needed.

'I'm so sorry,' she was saying. 'I've really screwed up, haven't I? I'm a little light on details but I do remember you. You like the ocean too. And we played together as children. You and me and another boy.'

'Jared.' She couldn't even remember Jared.

'Yes. Jared. Jared, my...'

Trig waited. Lena frowned.

'Brother,' he told her, because he couldn't stand the confusion in her eyes.

'Right. I'm pretty sure the concussion's screwing with my head.'

'You think?' Sarcasm didn't become him, given the circumstances, but it was that or outright panic. She'd barely touched her food. He'd hardly made a dent in his and he shovelled another load down, because he didn't rule out another trip to the hospital in the not too distant future.

'You should try and eat something,' he said gruffly, and she speared a small chunk of baked eggplanty stuff and ate it. Usually if he suggested she eat more, she'd tell him in no uncertain terms that she didn't tell him what to eat.

Lena's memory-lapse problem was worse than he thought.

He needed to get her upstairs and resting.

He needed to stop totally freaking out.

'We're after platinum rings,' she said suddenly. 'With a brushed finish.'

What did he even *say* to that?

'And carpet. I wanted one of those too.'

'A silk one,' he said, and condemned himself to hell for his sins.

'Expensive?'

'Oh, yes.'

'And you had a...problem with that?' she continued tentatively.

'Not at all. I'm thinking we need two.' And a brain transfusion. For him.

'Are we rich?' She wasn't even pretending to remember stuff any more.

'Between us, we have resources.' He thought that was a relatively fair call. 'And your father's a very rich man.'

'I don't sponge off him, do I?'

'No, but you're used to a certain way of life. You and your siblings all travel wherever you want, whenever you want to. You have several family houses and apartments at your disposal.'

'But the beach house is ours. I remember the beach house.'

'That's Damon's.'

'Oh.' Lena's face fell and she blinked back sudden tears. 'Could have sworn it was ours.'

'We've spent a lot of time there lately,' he offered gruffly. 'There's an indoor heated pool there that's good for rehab. You've done a lot of rehab on your leg.'

'Oh,' she said again.

Trig set his napkin on the table and pushed away abruptly. 'C'mon. I've had enough and you need to rest.'

She tried to follow swiftly. She caught her hip on the edge of the table and winced.

'Easy, though. There's no rush.'

'Nothing works,' she whispered.

'It works. It just works different from the way you expect it to.'

She clutched at his arm and together they headed slowly for the lifts. 'Do I have a crooked wooden walking stick?'

'Yes.'

'Did you give it to me for when you weren't around?'

'Yes.'

'Thought so.'

The lift door opened and they stepped in. Lena

didn't release his arm when he thought she would. The old Lena wouldn't have taken his arm at all. He looked at the picture they made in the mirror, she was looking at the picture they made too, and her eyes were like bruises. He'd wanted this—them—for so long, but not like this. He needed the old Lena back before he pursued this.

'I must have a really excellent personality,' she said.

'Why's that?'

'Look at you.'

He eyed himself warily. Same oversized buffoon who'd failed to protect Lena. Again.

'You look like a Hollywood action hero.' She frowned when he didn't reply. 'You're not, are you?'

'Pass.'

'Professional athlete?'

'No.'

'Fireman? I hear those boys lift a lot of weights in their spare time?'

'Where'd you hear that?'

'So you *are* a fireman?'

'No.'

She stood there in silence, but not for long. 'So what *do* you do? A wife should probably know.'

'I work for Australia's Special Intelligence Service.'

'You're a spy? Are you *serious*?'

'You work for them too.'

The lift doors opened and before Lena could protest, Trig lifted her into his arms and headed for the room. She'd done enough walking for the day and maybe, just maybe, he needed to hold her for a little while and pretend that she was safe.

'Do you carry me often?' she asked as she wound her arms around his neck and relaxed into his arms.

'As often as I can.'

And then Lena pressed her face to the hollow of his neck and took a deep breath and her arms tightened around him.

'I remember this,' she murmured. 'I remember the way you smell.'

Trig didn't need to die and go to hell. Hell had come to him.

She pressed a tentative kiss to his neck and his arms tightened around her. 'Why do I call you Trig?'

'Because I tutored you in trigonometry back in high school.'

'So, I needed help. Meaning I'm not exactly a scholar.'

'Depends on the company. You topped your state in mathematics, which for most seventeen-year-old girls is an excellent result. You just happen to have a couple of geeky geniuses in the family. It skews your expectations.'

'I sound insecure.'

She *was* insecure. More so since East Timor. She just couldn't get it through her head that her family cherished her for who she was. That her common sense and iron will often carried *them*.

They'd reached the door and Trig set her down reluctantly and opened it. His bag stood just inside the door, he'd had the hotel staff shift it from last night's room back to this one. The doctor had said to monitor Lena through the night. He'd figured he could do that better from her room than from his. At that point he'd still been under the impression that Lena *knew* she wasn't his wife.

She looked at the two beds and slanted him a sideways glance. 'Not exactly the honeymoon suite. Or the Ritz.'

'Yeah, about that...' Was *now* the right time to tell her that they weren't married or would that news only confuse and alarm her more? Did he let her sleep on it and hope to hell she woke up with her memory back?

Who the hell knew?

'Sometimes your leg bothers you and you need the extra space to stretch out. And tonight, for example, what with your head and your leg and the fact that you really don't remember me...it's probably a relief to you that we have twin beds tonight, right?'

She didn't say 'right,' she said 'oh,' and for a moment looked utterly lost.

'So, your gear's all here,' he continued doggedly and gestured towards the cupboard and her suitcase. 'I, ah, can run you a bath while I have a quick shower. The bath takes a while to fill.'

'No bath,' she said. 'I'll shower after you and then jump into bed. This bed.' She pointed to the one nearest the window. Trig nodded and slung his bag on the other one and rifled through it for clean underwear and a T-shirt and sweats. He needed a shower and a lot more distance from Lena than was currently available, but sometimes a man had to take what he could get.

He reached for the shutter divider between bathroom and bedroom.

'Can you not?' Lena asked hurriedly.

'What?'

'I mean, you can shut them, of course you can. But if you wanted to leave them open you could do that too. It's just…I feel better when I can see you.'

How could he possibly close them after that?

He left them open. He walked around the other side of that half wall and into the bathroom and shucked his clothes quickly, no showing off allowed. He didn't want Lena looking and wondering. He most emphatically didn't want her coming and touching.

Much.

He stepped into the shower before he'd even turned on the taps. He washed away the stench of fear and let icy resolve replace it. He could offer Lena comfort and reassurance tonight. He'd spent plenty of nights in the chair beside her hospital bed—tonight would be a lot like that, what with Lena wounded and aching and him half worried out of his brain. They'd done this before. Nothing to sweat about.

Except for the bit where *she thought he was her husband*.

Nothing to sweat about at all.

Lena opened her suitcase while her husband took the longest shower in the history of mankind. She really wanted to see him when he emerged, slick with water and minus a towel. She figured that particular image ought to be engraved on her brain, concussion or not, but unfortunately she had no memory of it.

She found her toiletries bag amongst her clothes and opened it up and found all sorts of yummy things. Lovely brand-name make-up. A travel-sized bottle of rose-scented perfume, and she popped the cap and lifted it to her nose with the thought that a familiar scent might jog a few memories back into place, and it did, for she had a brief flash of a laughing dark-haired woman wearing a totally awesome headband full of feathers.

'Do I know a Ruby?' she asked as she stoppered the perfume and returned it to the toiletries bag.

'Damon's wife,' came the rumble from the shower cubicle. 'Ruby's cool.'

'Does she buy me perfume?'

'She takes you frock shopping, for which I'm eternally grateful. She may have bought you perfume—I can't say for sure.'

'Why are you grateful?' Lena couldn't seem to find any frocks at all amongst the clothes she'd brought. These clothes ran more to casual trousers and tops that wouldn't need ironing.

'Ruby's totally committed to bringing sexy back. I heartily approve.'

Lena rifled through her clothes again and lifted out the plainest pair of white cotton panties that she'd ever seen. What kind of woman took *these* on her honeymoon? 'Maybe you should have married her.'

'Nah. She can't surf. Or hang-glide. Or put a bullet in a moving car wheel from half a kilometre away.'

'And I can?'

This time he hesitated before answering. 'You used to be able to. Little bit different now.'

She couldn't remember any of that, but the notion that she'd once done all that didn't particularly alarm her, so maybe it was true. 'So how did I get all the scars? And the bad leg?'

The water cut off abruptly. Moments later the top half of Trig appeared, framed in the cutaway wall. Water ran off him in rivulets and muscle played over bone as he reached for a towel and set it to his face and then scrubbed his hair with it. She couldn't see anything below mid waist, but even so...

All that sun-bronzed, spectacularly muscled glory and it was *hers*.

How in hell had she managed that?

'You don't remember what happened to your leg?' he said when his face re-emerged from beneath the towel and the towel drifted lower. Never had a woman been more resentful of a wall.

'No.'

'You got shot. On a mission. Nineteen months ago. You've made a spectacular recovery, given the prognosis.'

'What was the prognosis?'

'A wheelchair.'

Oh. Well, then... 'Good for me.'

'Good for us all.'

His clothes went on and she mourned the loss of skin. She wondered if he wore PJs to bed and hoped he did not.

'Shower's free,' he said on his way out and if that wasn't a hint for her to wash away the smell of the street and the hospital, nothing was.

'I'm getting there.' She was. 'But I can't find my honeymoon nightie. Do you have it?'

Trig opened his mouth as if to speak and then shut it again with a snap. He shook his head. No.

She looked beneath the pillows. 'Did we rip it?'

Still no sound from Trig.

'Could be the cleaner mistook it for ribbon,' he said at last.

'Ribbon?'

'There wasn't much of it. But there were bows. Lots of bows. Made out of ribbon.'

'Oh.' Lena tried to reconcile ribbon nightwear with the rest of her clothing. 'I really should be able to remember that.'

She passed her husband on the way to the shower and when she stepped beneath the spray she could have sworn she heard him whimper. So she'd screwed up their honeymoon by falling prey to a gang of pickpockets. She couldn't have been much of an operative—they were probably glad to be rid of her.

She contemplated washing her hair and decided it could wait. Her hair took for ever to dry, the bump on her head was starting to ache and she wanted nothing more than to fall into bed in the arms of her husband and burrow into his warmth until she fell asleep. Tomorrow would be a better day. Tomorrow she'd have her memory back and they might even be able to continue on to wherever it was they were going.

It could have been worse. She might not have been married to a wonderful man who knew exactly how to take quiet control of hospital staff and taxi drivers and her.

She could have been alone.

Trig had set his laptop up at the table by the time Lena emerged from the shower, scrubbed pink and wrapped in a fluffy white towel. She rifled through her suitcase, but couldn't seem to find whatever she was looking for.

'What was I *thinking*?' she grumbled, and disappeared back into the bathroom with a little grey T-shirt and a pair of yellow-and-white-striped boyleg panties in hand.

Trig sent up silent thanks for small mercies given that she hadn't dropped towel in front of him, and went back to surfing the net for local news, more specifically what had been happening in the port city of Bodrum on Turkey's southwest coast. It killed the time. It could prove useful. And it gave him something to do while Lena prepared for bed.

Because Lena preparing for bed involved her sitting on the bed and applying scented lotion to every millimetre of visible skin. It involved the brushing of hair—and working gently around the bump on her head and it involved the gentle lift and fall of her breasts and slender arms as she wove her hair into a long loose plait that he immediately wanted to undo, much like the imaginary ribbon nightgown that he also wanted to undo.

Eventually, Lena slid between the sheets, but she didn't lie down and the torture continued. She had pillows to divvy out and covers to turn down and Trig had no idea what was in the email he'd just read.

'Will you be much longer?' she asked, and he looked up to find her looking at him, her glorious grey-blue eyes full of silent entreaty.

He could be misreading her.

But he didn't think so.

'Why?' he croaked, and cleared his throat and tried again. 'Is the light bothering you? I still have some work to get through, but I can turn off the room lights, no problem.' Maybe he wouldn't covet what he couldn't see. Worth a try. 'It's a backlit screen. I can keep working.'

'I know you said we sometimes sleep in different beds but could you come to this bed tonight when you're done?'

'Yeah,' he said. 'Sure.' And vowed to wait until she was asleep before going anywhere near that bed and the temptation within it.

She lay back against the pillows, with her head to one side, carefully avoiding the bump on the back of her head. She let out a little sigh that did nothing whatsoever for his calm. 'Good?' he asked gruffly.

'Heaven.'

'Close your eyes.'

'Why?'

'I have it on good authority that you'll sleep better if you do.'

'How about a trade? I'll close them if you come and hold me.'

What was a husband to do?

So he lay down atop the covers, on his side, and pushed her hair away from her face with fingers too big and clumsy for the job, but she smiled at him, so he stroked the pad of his thumb against her cheek bone, rough against silky soft and smooth, and she made a little hum of pleasure and tilted her face towards his touch.

'Pretty sure I need a good-night kiss,' she mumbled, her eyes at half-mast already. 'You should probably get onto that before I fall asleep.'

She was wounded. He could do this. He pressed an almost-there kiss to the very corner of her mouth. The whole thing took maybe a couple of seconds.

'That's not a kiss.'

'Yeah, it is.'

'It's not a honeymoon kiss.'

'The honeymoon's on hiatus.'

'Seems a shame.'

'You need to get better first. Get your memory back.' And then, technically, they needed to get married.

'I can't remember your kisses.' She reached up and traced the curve of his lips with her fingertips. 'I want to.'

He'd never kissed her full on the mouth before. He'd always aimed for brotherly, and nailed it. Cheek kisses were good—they encouraged restraint. He and Lena had never practised anything *but* restraint when it came to kissing.

'Just one,' she murmured, her eyes grave on his.

'Lena—'

'It's not every day a woman gets to repeat her first kiss.'

'You can't remember *any* kisses?'

'Nope. First kiss. Going once... Going twice...'

Oh, hell.

He didn't wait to be asked a third time. He did try and do their first kiss justice—starting slow, keeping his hunger in check. No tongue, just the press of his lips against hers and those lips of hers were warmer and more willing than he'd ever imagined, and soft... so soft...

No tongue whatsoever until she flicked at the seam of his lips and tempted them open, and curled her tongue around his. And then he slanted his lips and deepened the kiss just a little. He tried to quieten her slick, darting tongue with the long slow slide of his as he learned her taste and committed it to memory. He tried to ignore just how well that smart mouth of hers matched his, but it fitted—it fitted so perfect and true that he lost himself for a moment, just surrendered all thought and took what he'd always wanted.

Lena couldn't believe she'd forgotten this man's kisses. Because they were everything she'd ever imagined kisses would be, from that first slow sweet slide to the all-consuming hunger that raced through her now. They'd done this before. How else could it be so perfect?

She'd known he was a big man—her memory might be faulty but there was nothing wrong with her eyes. What she hadn't understood was how much she gloried in his size and all that ruthlessly controlled strength looming over her. So much of him to explore and she wrenched her lips away from that too knowing mouth and set lips and teeth to his jaw instead.

A shudder swept through him and he groaned, more responsive than she could have ever dared wish for. She turned her lips to the strong cords of his neck and he cursed, even as he urged her closer.

'*Now* I remember why I married you,' she whispered against his skin and he trembled some more.

'Lena—'

'Mmm?'

'Lena, *please.*' Anyone would think she was torturing him. 'You have to stop. *I* have to stop. *Please.*'

Oh, he begged so *pretty.* A hot lick of power rushed over her, and she wondered what else he might beg for. What she might demand of him if she but had the courage to ask.

He kissed her again, hard and fast and ruthless, and then he was off the bed with a speed that surprised her, looking everywhere but back at her as he found his phone and slid those giant feet into his shoes. 'You need to rest and recover,' he muttered and headed for the door. 'And I need to make a couple of calls.'

SIX

—

Trig paced the length of the hall as he waited for Damon to pick up. He didn't want to talk to Damon, he wanted Damon's wife Ruby on the other end of the line, but there was a protocol involved when ringing up someone else's wife in the middle of the night and Trig wanted to observe it.

'This better be good,' said Damon when he finally picked up.

'It is. Put Ruby on. I need her advice.'

'About what?'

'You don't want to know.'

'I do want to know.'

'Your sister took a fall today and hit her head.'

'I'm putting you on speaker phone.' Nothing but tight concern in Damon's voice now.

'She's had an MRI and the doctors saw nothing to concern them. They've released her from the hospital, but she has concussion and some memory loss.'

He paused and wondered how best to deliver this next bit. 'She thinks we're married.'

He thought he heard scuffling and Ruby's low laughter, and then Ruby's voice came through warm and smoothly amused. 'How did that happen?'

'Lena had no ID when we got to the hospital and I had all mine. Easier to claim her and get her in front of a doctor and think about other consequences later. Ruby, she doesn't even remember Jared. She thinks we're on our honeymoon. She's back in the room. She thinks we share a bed! Do you have any idea how much I *want* to share that bed?' His voice had risen an octave or two.

'Touch my sister under those conditions and I will gut you,' said Damon.

'Don't threaten him,' muttered Ruby. 'How is that helpful?'

'He doesn't need to threaten me. If I take her now, I'll gut *myself*. She keeps getting me to hold her, Ruby. She wants the reassurance. She thinks she's my *wife*. You're a wife. What do I do?'

'You hold her, you moron.'

'Dead moron,' added Damon.

'What if she doesn't get her memory back? What if she wakes up in the morning and still thinks she's Mrs Lena Sinclair?'

'Got a nice ring to it,' said Ruby.

'Not helping.'

'Trig, sweetie. If Lena still thinks she's married to you in the morning, head on home to the beach house and we'll meet you there. Stay married, at least in Lena's eyes. Bring her home. That's my advice.'

'I can do that.'

'We know you can. That's why no one here is pacing around the room like a lunatic.' Ruby's voice had softened. 'Adrian, honey, give Lena a cuddle if she needs one—no one's going to castrate you for that, not even Lena when her memory returns. Just don't let the fairy tale get out of hand. Tell her you want to wait until she's fully recovered before you initiate marital relations. That's the truth anyway, isn't it? There has to be *some* reason you haven't made your move yet.'

'Does fear of rejection count?'

'We all own that one,' said Ruby dryly. 'Don't go thinking you're special.'

'Not special,' he said.

'But very worthy,' said Ruby quickly. 'Just because you shouldn't be making your move on Lena *now*, doesn't mean you shouldn't be making one at all. Move, by all means. We all want to see that.'

'You do?' He'd never really broached the subject of his feelings for Lena with any of her siblings before, but he wanted their approval. Jared's most of all. 'You speaking for Damon now too?'

'Yes,' said Damon. 'And Damon's speaking for the family.'

'That include Jared?'

'Proxy vote,' said Damon. 'Jared's not here.'

'I suggest you let Lena deal with Jared in the unlikely event that he objects to you courting her,' said Ruby. 'The man owes her.'

'For what?'

'Disappearing. Putting vengeance before family.' Ruby's voice had cooled considerably, but Ruby's father had disappeared without a trace too. Ruby knew what it felt like to be one of the ones they left behind. 'Brother Jared needs to spend some time in the naughty corner when he finally reappears.'

The words *if he reappears* went unspoken but Trig heard them anyway. 'You could suggest it to him,' he muttered. 'Although, fair warning, Jared doesn't take too kindly to reprimand.'

'So I've heard,' said Ruby, and then she yawned.

Damn but she could make him grin. 'I want front-row tickets to your first meeting with Jared. And popcorn.'

'Get in line,' said Damon. 'Take care of my sister. You've got this. I trust you.'

A substantially calmer Trig returned to the room and closed the door quietly behind him. He took a deep breath and searched for some of that steely resolve that everyone else seemed to think he had an endless supply of. He headed for the beds and for Lena who was in one of those beds, hurt and confused and...

Fast asleep.

SEVEN

—

Tuesday morning broke with the sound of the dawn prayer. Istanbul, thought Lena. I'm in Istanbul with its mosques and its rich cultural history and its slick market thieves. Her head throbbed when she moved it ever so slightly—time for more painkillers. There they were on the bedside table with a glass of water beside them, two of them, ready to go.

She eased up onto her elbow and reached for them with her spare hand, and then reached for the water to wash them down with. Give it five or ten minutes and the throbbing would stop and the fog would take over, fog being preferable to pain on most occasions, both of them preferable to being dead.

She rolled over, careful not to lie on the lump on her head, and there was Trig, next to her on the bed, faint shadows beneath his eyes and those long girly lashes. He looked younger in sleep and his body was even bigger up close.

He was still the most beautiful man she'd ever seen.

The urge to touch him became unbearable and she scooted closer and slid her hand across his chest. She'd have plastered herself against the rest of him only he'd slept on top of the covers rather than between them. Five more minutes, maybe ten, and the throbbing would stop and maybe she'd be able to do something about waking him in ways a man on his honeymoon might want to be woken, but for now just resting her cheek on his shoulder would do.

And then he rolled towards her and the covers got shoved to the bottom of the bed as he gathered her close and wrapped his arms around her. Target acquired, mission accomplished, and with the faintest rumbling sigh he slid straight back into sleep.

Five more minutes, she thought as she burrowed into his warmth. Five more minutes.

Or maybe an hour.

Trig woke slowly, with Lena wrapped around him like a limpet and strands of silky black hair tickling his jaw. She stirred as soon as he shifted, and snuggled in closer even as he tried to draw away.

'Lena—' Somehow, one of his hands had made its way to her waist. The other one had journeyed a little lower. Neither hand was in any hurry to let go. 'Lena, I need to get up.'

'No, you don't.'

'I really do.' He pressed a brief kiss to her shoulder and then peeled himself out of there, one reluctant limb at a time. 'What do you want for breakfast?'

'You.'

She still had her eyes closed. She'd rolled over into his warm spot, tucked her arms beneath his pillow and probably wasn't awake enough to know what she was saying.

'And some of that yoghurt you got me yesterday. And the tea,' she mumbled into the pillow.

'So you do remember.'

'It was good tea.'

'About the man and wife thing...'

'I know,' she murmured. 'Who wants a wife who gets beat up on the first day of their honeymoon? I'm a bad wife. Already. But I will make it up to you. Promise. Just as soon as I get up and go shopping.'

So much for Lena waking up this morning with her memories intact. 'I really think you should rest,' he said. And he'd book those flights. 'Shopping can wait.'

'Wrong.' She rolled onto her back and fixed him with a sleepy gaze. 'Have you *seen* the clothes in my suitcase? No. And you're not going to. They're funeral clothes. I brought the wrong suitcase.'

'You have a funeral suitcase?'

'I must have. There's no other explanation.'

'Pretty sure I can think of one. You want to hear it?'

'No, I want to shop. And eat yoghurt,' she pleaded wistfully. 'And pastry. Lots of flaky breakfast pastry. I'm starving.'

Now he was starving too.

'Lena, do you remember where you are?'

'Istanbul.'

'Do you know why you're here?'

'Honeymoon.'

Okeydokey, then. Time for another trip to the hospital. 'You want me to get you anything else while I'm out?'

'Yes,' she said. 'Champagne and strawberries.'

Five hours later, the doctor declared the swelling in Lena's head much reduced and Trig had declared her memory much improved. She could talk about Damon, Poppy and her father with assurance. She could talk about Jared and the things they'd done in the past. But she had no recollection of getting shot in East Timor, or of her long and arduous recovery, or of Jared going rogue in order to find out who'd betrayed them.

She still thought she was Mrs Lena Sinclair.

The doctor had nixed any long-haul flights for Lena for the next few days, but all was not lost.

The doctor had also banned sex.

'Got it,' he'd told the doctor swiftly. 'No sex. Plenty of rest. Doctor's orders.'

And then Lena had turned accusing eyes on him and it would have been flattering and funny if it hadn't been so tragic.

They'd returned to the hotel and Lena had obediently dozed for a couple of hours before declaring herself completely over the hotel-room experience and desperate to take a slow, relaxing walk through the hippodrome next to the Blue Mosque.

'Is this a honeymoon thing?' he asked suspiciously.

Because it sounded like a honeymoon thing and he wanted to avoid those.

'It's a tourist thing.'

'The doctor said you had to rest.'

'And I have. Now I need to do something.'

'The walking will tire you.'

'How about a Turkish bath, then? Warm water. Relaxation. I hear they even throw in a massage.'

'Water baby.'

'I do recall a fondness for water. And doing a lot of leg rehab in it.' Lena frowned. 'You said I got shot in the line of duty. I still don't remember a thing.'

'Lucky you.'

'Can you describe it to me?'

'No.'

She looked at him with far too penetrating a gaze and he thought she would push the issue, but then she shrugged and rifled through her suitcase and held up a brightly coloured swimsuit. 'So...Turkish bath or unwanted interrogation? Which will it be?'

Which was how they ended up at a Turkish bath house, with him being shepherded through a door to the left labelled men and Lena being pointed to the one on the right that said women.

'Wait for me when you get out,' he commanded gruffly.

'Don't I always?'

Surprisingly, upon reflection, the answer was yes. He gave her a grin. 'Rest and relaxation,' he said. 'Don't forget.'

'I'm on it.'

Once through the man door, an attendant showed him to a shower cubicle and change room. 'You must shower first,' the attendant said. 'And then this door will take you into the bathing area.'

Trig nodded. There'd been pictures of the bath house on the waiting room walls. Rooms full of marble and cascading water. Huge stone slabs where bodies lay prone and masseuses worked their magic. Enough steam to make a belching dragon proud.

Lena's post-op physiotherapy programme had involved a lot of water-based stretching and exercises and whether she remembered those exercises or not, a warm bathing pool and massage would be good for her.

Trig showered and stowed his wallet and clothing in the locker provided. He picked up a tiny square face cloth from a carefully folded pile of them sitting at the door to the bathing area. No swimwear required, apparently. It said so, right there on the instructions plaque hanging on the wall.

The first thing his eyes were drawn to as he stepped into the room was the high domed and tiled ceiling. The second thing he saw was Lena entering through a door on the other side of the room.

Why on earth would a bathing house have separate change-room areas when the bathing area was for males and females both?

Like him, Lena had only one cloth.

And she didn't seem to know where to put it.

Only half a dozen other people swam or lazed beneath the cascading water pouring from spouts in the wall. A few men. A few women. No one seemed to be paying much attention to anyone else.

Didn't matter. Lena stood butt naked with one tiny little cloth that she seemed to want to cover the worst of her scarring with. He crossed to her quickly and held out his cloth.

'Here. Use it. Cover yourself up.'

She seemed to find his glower amusing. 'Which bits? Because these wash cloths? Really not that big.'

'Get in the pool,' he ordered. The pool would provide at least some protection against prying eyes. And they *were* drawing attention. He could feel eyes boring into his back. 'You'd think they might have mentioned when we came in that this was a mixed bathing pool.'

Lena was making her way slowly down the steps, holding fast to the hand rail. 'Relax,' she said. 'This is working for me. Are you sure you don't want your flannel back? Or mine as well, for that matter. Because, frankly, most of the women and some of the men in here are staring at you and salivating.' Her lashes swept over her eyes and she scanned him from head to toe. 'And why wouldn't they? There's a lot to love.'

He followed her down into the water fast. He'd never considered himself body shy, but still... 'Keep the flannels. *Use* the flannels. Why aren't you freaking out?'

'Too busy watching you,' she said with a grin, and

then slid into the water and struck out for the far side of the pool. 'Oh, this is nice.'

'Wouldn't you be more comfortable if you were, oh, I don't know...not buck naked?'

'Adrian Sinclair.' Her voice floated warm and teasing across the water. 'Are you self-conscious?'

'Apparently.' The water was deliciously warm, bordering on hot. Lena would like it. 'I'm also possessive—particularly where you're concerned. And I'm on my honeymoon and all kinds of frustrated. You might want to keep this in mind should the masseur attempt to wash you down.' The masseur was washing someone down on the marble block now, and there were suds, lots of suds, and a wet white towel that the masseur was scouring the skin with. He wasn't being gentle. 'Maybe you should give that experience a miss, because if he scrubs too hard and antagonises your scars I'll have to relieve him of his arms.'

'I'm sure he'll adjust his ministrations accordingly.'

Trig watched as the masseur fisted half the towel around his hands and proceeded to bring the free end of the towel down hard on the person's back. He did it again and the towel landed lower this time. Again and again, all the way down to the toes. Every time the towel came down the body strung out on the slab twitched.

'I might give the flagellation a miss,' said Lena after a moment.

The masseur had downed the towel and picked up a huge bucket full of water. For someone so small and wiry, the man had some serious body strength. Next minute, he'd thrown the entire contents of the bucket at the person lying on the slab.

'Wasn't expecting that,' said Lena as the person sat up, a man, now that you could see past the suds. The front of him got slammed with another full bucket of water and then he stood up and headed towards a nearby waterfall of water and half disappeared under it. 'You reckon that was cold water?'

'Yes.'

'Me too.'

She had such a shameless grin. 'You going to tell me how I got these scars now? Because I think I'm ready to hear it. It bothers me that I can't remember if this happened because I did something wrong.'

'You did nothing wrong.'

'I don't suppose you could expand on that?'

'I don't want to discuss it.'

'Trig, I look at my body in the mirror and I see the scars and feel the aches but I don't know how they got there. It's really disconcerting, and I'd really like to know. I appreciate that it's probably not a memory that you want to revisit, but please...'

Trig scrubbed his hand over his face. He had no defences against a pleading Lena. None.

'So we were on a simple recon run in East Timor,' he began. 'There'd been a last-minute change of plans and we got asked to check out an old chemical weapons lab that had been reported abandoned about three years earlier. That's what the mission profile said. We came in careful, we always do, and found cobwebs and dust. No footprints. No sign of use. No equipment on the benches, nothing in the cupboards. The place had been picked clean and left to rot.

'We came back outside. Didn't figure we had a problem until semi-automatic fire came at us from the left flank and took you down. I don't know why, because there was nothing there to protect. Another two minutes and we'd have been out of there. No activity to report. Not coming back.'

'Did we catch the shooter?'

'No.'

'Do we have any idea who did the shooting?'

'No. And no rebel group put their hand up for it. The incident's been buried. No press coverage, nothing but an internal memo or two and a verdict of random opportunistic insurgence.'

'You don't sound convinced.'

'I'm not. There's something else going on. Jared's looking into it. Quietly.'

Lena nodded. Trig waited.

But no memories of Lena coming to Turkey specifically to find Jared were forthcoming.

Lena leaned her head back against the tiled lip of the pool and closed her eyes. 'Think I'm going to forget the scrub-down altogether and stay right here for at least an hour. The only thing I plan on opening my eyes for is to watch you get all sudsed up and sluiced back down. I could appreciate that show a lot.'

'Never going to happen.'

'Probably for the best. If it did, I'd want a way of showing ownership and you're not wearing a ring. By the way, when *are* we getting our rings? Because I have some more ideas on what I'd like.'

'You do?'

'I do. And I found a wad of cash and a couple of credit cards in my suitcase belonging to one Lena West. I can pay for rings.'

'Gentleman pays for the rings, Lena.'

'Since when?'

'Pretty sure it's a rule.'

'Do we follow rules? As a rule.'

'Always. What sort of wedding ring do you want?'

'Plain brushed platinum. Wide.'

'You want diamonds in it?'

'Meh.'

'What about a diamond engagement ring?'

'Shouldn't I already have one of those?' Lena frowned. 'I wish I could remember your proposal. I want to know how you got away with not giving me a ring.'

'It's possible I promised you the world instead.'

'Not the moon and the stars?'

'Those too. And Saturn's rings.'

'Classy,' she murmured. 'Were we beneath the stars at the time?'

Trig made an executive decision. 'We were on the beach, lying in the whitewash watching baby turtles hatch and return to the sea and it was a starry, starry night.'

'I can see how that would work. Where would you have even put a ring?'

'Exactly.'

'I could have a turtle engraved on the inside of mine,' she murmured.

Or not.

'Or the date.'

Or not.

'What *was* the date of our wedding?'

'November the twenty-eighth.'

'I've been married almost a week already? Doesn't feel like a week.' She favoured him with a sultry smile. 'You really are going to have to bed me soon. Because it's criminal that I can't remember any of that.'

'You can't help it. No need to dwell on it. I'm not dwelling on it.'

'I can't remember any of the sex we had before marriage, either. That's assuming we had it.'

'Lena, can we *not* talk about the sex we may or may not have had? I am stark naked in a public bathing pool and at some point I am going to have to get out of here without giving anyone here a heart attack.'

'You want your wash cloth back?'

'No! Keep the cloth. You need that cloth to cover *you* up when we get out of here.'

'This isn't working for you, is it? You're not relaxing.'

'Maybe if we stopped *talking*.'

She lasted less than five minutes. Five minutes during which he convinced himself that if he took nothing too seriously, he could probably get through another day of being married to Lena without losing his mind.

'So would *you* wear a brushed-platinum wedding band?' she asked.

'Yes.' Not a lie. More of a theoretical answer to a theoretical question.

'There could be a glossy strip running through it like a wave. And there could be diamonds, little ones, like a little wavy strip crosswise across the band. Or little sapphires the colour of the sea. But not the deep blue sea. The light blue sea.'

'I see.' And he did.

'Maybe we should consult a jewellery designer.'

'Maybe. Are you tired?' he asked. 'I'm tired.'

'Hot water does that. May I ask you another question that I can't remember the answer to?'

'Shoot.'

'It's December the fourth already and we're in Turkey on our honeymoon. How long is our honeymoon going to take and where are we going for Christmas?'

'That's two questions.' And he didn't know the answer to either. 'Two weeks for the honeymoon—though if your memory doesn't reappear in all its glory soon I want to cut this trip short and take you home.'

Lena said nothing.

'I mean it, Lena.'

'I know you do. I can hear it in your voice.' She brought her hands to the surface of the water and started churning slow circle patterns in the froth. 'I'm remembering more. I can tell you that. I remember tagging after you and Jared when I was a kid and resenting the hell out of you both for being stronger, faster and more fearless than me. I remember wanting to rip Jessica's eyes out because you took her to your year twelve formal.'

'Really? You remember that?'

'As if it were yesterday. First time I'd ever seen you wearing a suit and tie and the things it did for your shoulders and my libido. As for Jessica, she had an hourglass figure, waist-length auburn hair and a smile just for you. In another universe I might have even liked her. She didn't even look at Jared.'

'Yeah, that was always a good sign in a date. Jessica was a good sport.' Who'd known by the end of the night that Trig didn't want to take things any further. 'Probably still is.'

'Jealous wife here,' warned Lena.

'You're a good sport too,' he offered hastily.

'Are you sure? Because I seem to recall that I really, really like to win.'

'This is true.'

'I also have this niggling suspicion that I'm a bad loser.'

'Sometimes you react badly when you're forced to reveal weakness in front of others,' he offered carefully. 'You hate that.'

'Well, who wouldn't?'

'Borrowing strength from someone else when you need it doesn't make you weak. Makes you human.' He laid out his thoughts for her; honest in a way he'd never been before. 'Sometimes I wish you'd lean on others a little more.'

'Doesn't that make me needy?'

'Not saying I want to tie your shoelaces for you. But when you're railing against your body's limitations and when you're scared about being left out or left behind, would it kill you to say something?'

'Like what? Carry me?'

'Something like that.'

'You've carried me before.'

'I have.'

'Which must give you a certain sense of self-worth.'

'I'm usually more focused on staying alive at the time.'

'Can't you see that me borrowing strength from others gives me less self-worth? That the last thing I want is to be a burden to you?'

'It's not like that. That's not what offering and receiving help is all about.'

'I hear you,' she said solemnly. 'I do, but, Adrian, ask yourself this: when has anyone ever carried you?'

Lena couldn't quite pinpoint the exact moment in the bath house when the conversation had turned from teasing to her pleading with Trig to understand her thoughts and feelings when it came to relying on others for things she ought to be able to do for herself.

She *did* rely on him when she needed to.

She'd relied on him yesterday—for memories and form-filling-out, for safety, and she'd let him carry her and rejoiced in the act; she remembered that part quite well. She was relying on him now, for information and companionship. What more did he want from her? Did she really try to hide her weaknesses from *him*?

They lasted an hour in the hot pool and beneath the cascading falls of water. There was a ledge you could lie on beneath one of the cascades and let the water beat down on you, and it did it with exactly the right amount of pressure. She made Trig try it but he preferred the more directed pressure of a side spout. Neither of them took up the masseuse's offer to soap them up and wash them down.

Maybe next time.

An hour and twenty minutes after they'd entered the bath house, they stepped out onto the street, squeaky clean and smelling ever so faintly of roses. Lena liked smelling of roses. She liked Trig smelling of roses too.

She came down the bath-house steps, feeling freer in her gait than she had been in days.

'You're walking easier.' He didn't miss much, this husband of hers.

'I know. Turkish baths are my new favourite place. And I know I suggested we look for rings after this, but I'm having second thoughts.' Never let it be said that she couldn't admit to weakness. She could work on that. Work on it right now. 'I'm tired, my head's beginning to throb and all I want to do is curl up on that hotel bed with a plate of fruit and a movie.'

'Lena West, are you admitting that you're not up to shopping with me?'

'I am. And I hope you're impressed and it's not Lena West. The name's Lena Sinclair.'

She did love a man with a wide and blinding smile.

They hailed a taxi and when they reached the hotel foyer they dropped by the restaurant and ordered a plate of fresh fruit and pastries, and hot coffee and tea to be brought to the room. She was getting used to this hotel now. The foyer and the lifts, the long walk from the lifts to the room.

She got halfway down the corridor before deciding she could use some more help. Especially if it involved being up close and personal with a husband who smelled ever so faintly of roses.

'Ouch,' she said and stopped. Trig stopped too. 'Could be I need a little more help.'

'With what?'

'Walking. I have this burning need to be in our room right now, and we'd get there a whole lot faster if you carried me.'

'Burning need, huh?'

'Scorching.'

He swung her into his arms. Damn, but she loved his smile. 'You feeling any less worthy there, princess?'

'No, I'm feeling kind of smug.'

'I've unleashed a monster.'

'Pretty sure I'll get the asking-for-help balance right eventually. Right now I'm feeling so breathless all of a sudden. I may need mouth-to-mouth.'

He got her to the door and got her inside.

And kissed her senseless.

The food arrived ten minutes later. Ten minutes during which her husband had avoided being on the bed with her for all he was worth, offered to run her another bath, twice, opened his computer and scowled at his emails and generally set her on edge with his inability to settle. He downed two cups of thick, fragrant coffee in rapid succession and stared at the walls as if contemplating climbing them.

'Got an email in from your brother,' he said finally.

'Jared?'

'Damon. He's got us seats on a flight out of here in three days' time.'

Lena sat up straighter so she could look her take-charge husband in the eye. 'What happens if my memory comes back before then?'

'Then I guess we cancel and continue on to Bodrum.'

'What's in Bodrum?'

He hesitated, just for a second. 'Boats.'

For the first time since waking up on the floor of Istanbul's Grand Bazaar, she wondered if her husband was lying to her.

'Seems like a long way to come for something I know we have a lot of at home.'

'Diving's not bad either.'

'Maybe if we were talking about Sharm El Sheik, down the bottom of the Sinai. Which we're not. We're talking about the Bosphorus.'

'Your geography's improving,' he murmured. 'That's got to be a good sign.'

Her spidey-sense was twitching too. Lena didn't know if that was a good thing or not.

'You're awfully worried about when I get my memory back, aren't you?'

Her husband's eyes grew carefully guarded. 'Not really.'

'Did we have a fight?'

'We often fight. Usually for no good reason.'

'So we *did* have a fight.'

'I didn't say that.'

'There's something you're not telling me. What don't I know?'

Trig ran a frustrated hand through his already dishevelled hair. 'I don't *know* what you don't know. Right now, I don't think *either* of us have a handle on what you do and don't know. There's stuff you're repressing.'

'The bad stuff?'

'Yeah. And I don't know how much of that to tell you right now, so I'm hedging, and waiting to see what does come back to you, and I'm stalling, for very good reasons, and hoping to hell that you'll wake up tomorrow morning and try and break my jaw, because then I'll *know* you're back.'

'Must've been some fight.'

'*We didn't fight.*'

'Then why can't I remember our wedding day? Why am I repressing that?' She suddenly felt nervous. More than nervous. 'Was it bad? For you? Was our wedding night a disaster?'

'God help me.'

'Tell me!'

'No.'

'No you won't tell me or no it wasn't a disaster?'

'It wasn't a *disaster*.'

'Do we have pictures of our wedding day?' Because she hadn't seen any on his laptop.

'I don't know about any pictures. We left right after...the thing.'

'The wedding.'

Trig nodded jerkily. 'Lena, can't you let it go? Just for now?'

'I can't.' She couldn't look at him any more. 'I can't remember our wedding day, or when you proposed to me or what we're like when we're together. Nothing, not even a flash, and of all the things I want to remember, it's those. It feels...disrespectful that I can't. Who forgets their own wedding?'

'It's not disrespectful.' Her cool, calm husband was unravelling fast.

'And we really are okay? We're not on the verge of divorce after a week?'

'No,' he said gruffly. 'No. Lena, I gotta get out of here for a bit. I'm going mad.'

'Will you look for wedding rings while you're out?'

'What?' The poor man looked positively hunted.

'Wedding rings. You could go browsing. Haggling. Blood sport.'

'I, uh, wasn't planning to.'

'Could you?' Anxiousness made her fidget. 'I mean, I wouldn't mind.' He'd told her to be clear about her fears. 'It'd give me something solid to hold to when I can't remember. Something real.'

She couldn't read him, this husband of hers. His face was all shut down and he stood so very still.

'You sure you wouldn't rather wait until your memory comes back?' She could barely hear him.

'I don't want to wait. I'd come with you—we can do it tomorrow if you'd rather not choose them on your own—but I don't want to wait. I trust you to choose well.'

Trig ran a big hand over his face.

'Trust you full stop,' she said, hoping to reassure him.

And somehow made it worse.

'I'll look,' he said hoarsely and handed over his laptop for her entertainment and fled as if the hounds of hell were snapping at his heels.

Lena let out a breath when the door snicked closed behind her husband. *Damn,* but she wished she could remember what had gone wrong between them. Because *something* had and she needed to know what so that she could fix it.

Restless, she turned to his computer and trawled through his music file, trying to find something she *didn't* thoroughly approve of.

Maybe he'd downloaded his entire music collection from her.

She scrolled though the photo files next and found plenty of her and Trig or her and Jared, or Jared and Trig—most of them involving ropes and sails and water. She saw pictures of her and Poppy in an elegant apartment and felt relatively certain that the apartment in the picture belonged to her father. She saw a picture of Damon giving surfing lessons to a buxom redhead wearing a buzzy-bee headband and knew it had to be Ruby.

Her memory was returning. Maybe not all at once, maybe in fits and starts, but it *was* coming back.

She trolled through Trig's video collection next. A couple of V8 car races that didn't interest her at all. Some big wave surfing footage that did. The entire season three of a local cooking show. Huh. And a TV miniseries about a circus, a drifter and a whole bunch of supernatural goings-on.

The creepy circus show won hands down.

She was still watching it four hours later when Trig returned. Well, maybe not watching it intently. It was entirely possible that she'd drifted off to sleep at some point between the first episode and wherever they were up to now. Daylight had come and gone. Dusk ruled the sky now.

Trig looked at her, looked at the computer screen.

'Relaxing,' he said.

She did like a man with a crooked smile. 'Doctor's orders.'

'You do know you've seen this before.'

'As far as I'm concerned, it's all new. And if this is

new, think what else could be an all-new experience.
I've been re-virginised.'

'Don't even go there.' Trig pointed a warning finger at her.

'Think about it. I've barely been kissed. My breasts
have never been tou—'

'*Lena!*'

'I love it when your voice gets all gruff and commanding.' She lay back on the bed, all biddable and
boneless. 'Who knew?'

'No sex. Doctor's orders.'

'Honeymoon,' she reminded him.

'You're just bored.'

This was true. 'So entertain me. What's new in the
land of out there?'

'Well, the shopping here is still an experience to
remember and I still pray for my life whenever I get
into a taxi. The taxi driver's name this time round
was Boris.'

'Did he know where to find the best wedding rings?'

'Of course he did. What kind of question is that?'

'And did you find any *you* liked?'

'You want to see?'

Lena sat up fast. Of course she wanted to see. 'What
kind of question is that?'

He put his hand in his jeans pocket, pulled out a
little velvet pouch and tossed it onto the bed.

Lena eyed the little pouch with extreme anticipation. 'Not that I don't appreciate the right-to-my-fingertips delivery but shouldn't you be on bended knee?'

'Couldn't you just think of the turtles?'

'I would if I could remember them. Bend. And give me the proposal speech.'

And wonder of wonders he went down on one knee and made Lena breathless.

'Heaven help me,' he said.

'Keep talking.'

'Okay.' He cleared his throat and swallowed hard. 'Okay, I can do this.'

'Hang on.' She smoothed back her hair and straightened her top, sat up straight, shoulders back and an imaginary book sitting on her head. No need for complacence just because they'd done this before. 'Ready.'

'Glad one of us is.'

'Take your time.'

He took a deep breath instead. 'We've known each other a long time,' he began raggedly. 'I've loved you for a long time. You're it for me. For better and for ever, there's nowhere else I'd rather be than at your side, so...Lena Aurelia West, will you marry me?'

Those weren't tears in her eyes. They *weren't*.

'Yes,' she said simply. 'Yes. I love you too.'

Trig let out a breath and Lena realised, belatedly, that he was nervous. Really nervous.

'Why are you shaking? You knew I'd say yes.' She closed the laptop and pushed it away. She reached out to her husband and coaxed him up onto the bed. 'That was so beautiful. You should do it again.'

'Once was enough.'

'Twice.'

'Right.'

'You look pale.'

'Probably fear.' He picked up the little royal-blue velvet pouch. It had silver writing on it that she didn't understand, that she didn't need to understand as he pried loose the string, took her hand, turned it palm up, and tipped three rings into it, two of them significantly smaller and more ornate than the third.

She picked up the first of the smaller rings. The brushed platinum had a glossy wave running through it. The second of the smaller rings was identical, except that this time the wave was a string of vivid blue sapphires, running from small to large and back to small again. Separate, they were beautiful. Together, on her finger, they looked superb.

'Real enough for you?' he asked.

'Yes.' They must have cost him a fortune.

She looked to the third ring. Brushed platinum, same as hers, but no wave ran through the thick plain band. She picked it up and studied the finish before reaching for his hand and pushing it onto his finger.

'Suits you,' she murmured. 'I'd have got you one with a wave as well. And I'd have been wrong. Have I mentioned lately, just how much I love your hands?'

'What?'

'Hands. Yours. I have a total fetish for them. Goes back years.'

'How many years?'

'You remember that kitten we found stuck in the drainpipe?'

'Yeah, but I remember the kitten's mother that found us two minutes later more. She *bit* me.'

'She did.' Lena grinned at the memory, for it was vivid, bright and *there*. 'You have a gentle touch, big guy. Even when under attack. That's when I fell for your hands.'

Her husband blushed, and Lena grinned some more. 'Truly, you're such a beautiful man, inside and out. I just wish I could remember what I did to deserve you. Because looking at you and then looking at me... Adrian, can I ask another question that you're not going to want to answer? Because it's a big one, and it's bugging me.'

'Can I reserve the right to not answer?'

'Where I got shot—there's so much scarring, so many hollows. Am I still able to have children?'

He didn't have to say a word; his eyes answered for him. Lena nodded and bit down hard on her lower lip. 'Okay.' She drew a ragged breath. 'Okay. *God.* I don't know what you see in me.'

'Don't you say that,' he said fiercely. 'Why do you *say* stuff like that? You're it for me. You always have been, and if you still want children, well, maybe we can't make one but we can care for one that needs caring for. Whatever you want to do, I'm in. All in. Promise me you'll remember that and that you'll remember this. Us. The way we are now.'

She straddled him because he was looking down at his wedding ring and she thought that he might bolt; she wrapped her arms around his neck and took his mouth with hers, gentle and coaxing at first, and then more languidly when he responded.

'Make love to me,' she whispered. She wanted that, wanted him inside her so damn much. 'We can go slow. Easy as breathing. The doctor couldn't possibly object to that.'

'We can't.' His hands were at her back and his lips were at her neck. '*I* can't. You need to get your memory back first.'

'For this?' His lips skated across her breastbone and sent a shaft of pure pleasure straight through her. 'Pretty sure I don't. I'm all for making new memories.'

'Lena, the doctor said no. You have a habit of ignoring doctor's orders.'

'Sounds about right.'

'It has a habit of backfiring.'

'Oh.'

He sat back against the headboard with Lena still on top of him. She leaned into him and he started drawing lazy lines across her back. Nice. As was the firmness still tightly lodged against her thighs. She rocked against him ever so gently. 'You going to take care of that?'

'It can wait. Tortured denial's my thing.'

'Really?'

'Apparently.' Those clever hands of his scratched at a spot behind her ear and almost set her to purring. 'Tomorrow,' he said, and it sounded like a prayer for salvation. 'Let's see how you're tracking tomorrow.'

* * *

He couldn't sleep. How was a man supposed to sleep when his head was full of the scent of the woman he loved and his heart was fair breaking under the weight of all the lies he'd just fed her. Not all of it lies: his proposal had been true. Lay his soul bare and hope Lena remembered in the morning.

See where this road led them and hopefully stumble across Jared along the way.

He still hadn't forgotten the real reason Lena was here, even if she had.

Because he could take Lena home the minute she was cleared to fly, and wait for her full memory to return, but the minute it did she'd be back out looking for her missing brother again.

He had half a mind to try and find Jared over the next couple of days, get Lena and her brother to sight each other and *then* take Lena home.

Trig slipped from the bed and reached for his T-shirt. He left the room with a mobile phone and minimum fanfare. The phone had come from Damon. Not government issue, nothing that could be traced back to him.

He punched in a number he knew off by heart and waited to see if a message bank would pick up the call. The message bank wasn't full and it should have been by now. Someone was clearing those calls. Hopefully it was Jared.

'Hey, man.' Jared would know who it was by the sound of his voice. If someone else had Jared's phone,

Trig didn't plan on making it any easier for them to identify him. 'Haven't seen you for a while and we're in the area so we're going to drop in. You owe me, big time. And you need to be there.'

EIGHT

———

Lena woke the next morning feeling clearer-headed than she had in days. Trig wasn't there—she remembered him rolling over and gathering her close and kissing her temple and then telling her he was heading out to get breakfast. She'd told him she'd come too, but she hadn't opened her eyes or properly woken up, and when she'd murmured something along the lines of five more minutes he'd told her it was five in the morning and to go back to sleep.

A command she'd been only too happy to follow.

So her husband was an early riser. She'd been an early riser too, back in the day when surfing had been an option, or sea kayaking had been an option. Kayaking might still be an option, come to think of it. Plenty of backwaters not too far away from Damon's beach house.

Or maybe it was time to get a pretty little cottage of her own, somewhere on the river. A cottage with panelled half-walls, high ceilings and bay windows.

A yesteryear cottage that cried out for Persian carpet runners and wide verandahs. Her family would think she'd gone nuts—but she could put an indoor bathing pool in one of the rooms if she got creative enough. She could fit it out like a Turkish spa.

She was still in that lovely dream place where anything was possible when Trig came back with breakfast. Strawberry yoghurt today, and mixed nuts and flaky pastry and some kind of spicy scrambled egg.

She sat up and pushed her tangle of hair away from her face. Every night she plaited it and tied it off with a hairband. Every morning the hairband had disappeared and the plait was a tangle. She hoped Trig liked the dishevelled look.

She should probably let him in on the granny cottage idea as well. 'Do you think any shops here sell marble water-spouts and feature walls? And tiles like the ones in the pool yesterday?'

'Why?' He handed her a cup of tea and bent down to place a fleeting kiss on the very edge of her lips.

'I want a Turkish bathing room in the cottage we're buying on the banks of a lazy river.'

'We're buying a cottage?'

'On the banks of a lazy river. So that I can get up and go kayaking and you can get up to no good with a tool belt.' Trig's father was a carpenter-builder. His older brother was a builder as well and Trig had spent many a school holiday with a tool belt strapped to his waist. Lena had the niggling suspicion that Trig's father resented the hell out of the Wests for leading Trig away from the family business.

'You want me to put on a tool belt?'

'Only when you're not out protecting national secrets. And if it's hot on the banks of that lazy river you can lose the shirt. I might even make a calendar of you looking like that. You could be Mr January all the way through to December.'

'Don't you dare.'

'Oh, I dare. You should know that by now.'

Her husband smiled his wide, happy smile. 'I've missed you,' he said, and then his gaze slid to the rings on her wedding finger and his smile dimmed. 'How's the head?'

'The bump is on its way down.' She took his hand and slid it through her hair. 'Feel.'

He did. Damn but he had a nice touch. She closed her eyes, tilted her head back and let him cradle the weight of it in that big hand of his. 'Mmm.'

He let her go in a hurry and retreated to the other side of the table.

'You are the shyest person I know when it comes to physical affection,' she told him grumpily.

'Doctor's orders.'

'I'm going back there today, just to get that particular directive lifted.'

'You still can't remember squat.'

'I'm remembering a little more each day. I'm on disability leave from work. And I just failed my physical.'

Trig grunted.

'I was a slow waddling duck for those pickpockets. ASIS isn't going to put me back in the field. Not sure I *want* to go back in the field if all I'm going to be is a liability. I need a new focus. Maybe a whole new career.' She eyed him curiously. 'Have you ever thought of quitting the business?'

'Not yet.'

'But you took a desk job.'

'You remember that?'

'Didn't you?'

'Yeah.' He rubbed at his temple.

'What's it like?'

'Lot of analysis.'

'Frustrating?'

Trig gave a reluctant nod.

'You could return to fieldwork.'

'What? And leave you all alone in the little house on the river? Who'd put the Christmas decorations on the roof?'

So he *had* altered his work focus because she'd been forced to alter hers. The confirmation gave her mixed feelings. On the one hand Lena was grateful that she was so well loved. On the other hand she was dismayed that he'd chosen to limit himself in order to be there for her. She wasn't that needy. Was she? 'You want to put Christmas decorations on the roof?' she asked lightly.

'I want Christmas decorations everywhere.'

Maybe it was time she expanded her earlier dream. 'I'm having second thoughts about the little house on the river. I think we need a big old farmhouse instead, with sheds to house all the toys and decorations when they're not being used. And if we're living on the river, I want a powerboat. A really fast one. I could take up speedboat racing.'

'Yeah, that's really going to encourage me to leave you there by yourself.'

'You could take up speedboat racing as well. I seem to recall having a quarter share in a plane that I could sell.'

'Handy,' he said dryly.

'Isn't it? I thought I might ring Jared today. Or Poppy. And I got a phone message in from someone only the name's not ringing any bells. Amos Carter.'

Trig frowned. 'Let me see it.'

She handed over her phone and Trig found the message and frowned some more.

'Who is he?'

'An old work contact.'

'Jericho3, Milta Bodrum Marina,' she said next. 'Is it a boat or a missile?'

'Don't know.'

'Are we curious?'

'I'm curious. Leave it with me. You're concussed.'

Lena sipped her tea. 'I still can't remember getting married.'

Trig eyed her sharply. Lena dropped her gaze. She wanted to. She was *trying* to.

'I guess what I'm saying is that if that particular memory stays elusive, I'd kind of like to do it all over again. The ceremony. Do you think the families would go for that?'

'I think your family would do anything for you. And mine could be persuaded along.'

'Would *you* do anything for me?'

'You really need to ask?' He held her gaze. Lena was the first to look away.

'So, yeah. That could happen,' he said gruffly. 'Get well and anything could happen.'

'You mean my leg.'

'Your leg is as good as it's ever likely to get. The kayaking and the speedboat racing are good options for you. I like that you're talking about them.'

'Promise me something. Promise you'll race me.'

Trig grinned and placed his hand to his mighty heart. 'Don't expect any quarter.'

'I'd take it as a grave insult if you gave me any. So what's the plan for today? I know you said we should go home if my memory stays faulty, but it *is* improving. I remembered that your father's a builder this morning. I remember you working his jobs in order to get the money to buy your surf kites. True or not true?'

'True.'

'So I'd like to stay. Maybe we could continue on with our honeymoon plans. Make the most of this time together, regardless.'

Trig looked to be on the verge of protest.

'After I've seen the doctor today and been given the all-clear, of course.'

'You're so amenable.'

'Aren't I always?'

Trig almost choked on his coffee. 'Yeah, no. I'm thinking it's a concussion side effect that has to do with a whole bunch of bad feelings that you can't remember.'

'But you prefer me amenable? You like this me better than you like the old me.'

Trig took his time answering. 'There's a few old yous. You as a kid. You as a comrade-in-arms. You trying to make your body work the way it did before, scared as hell that it wouldn't and even more scared of being cast aside by the people you love because of it. I had trouble getting that through to you. Fell in love with you even more because of it though. And then there's this you who's a whole lot like the old you— before the shooting—only softer somehow, and more assured. I could get used to this you too.'

'But which me do you love?'

'All of them.'

Good answer. 'So, assuming the doctor gives me the okay, where to next on the honeymoon trip?'

'Bodrum.'

'So you *do* know what Jericho3 is?'

'No,' he muttered. 'But I aim to.'

Lena got the all-clear to travel from the doctor and permission to back off on the medications. The doctor made a more thorough examination of the bruises on her hip this time around and made her show him what leg movement she had and asked her whether the pain there was any worse than before.

'No,' she assured him. 'That's about as good as it gets.'

The doctor nodded. 'You're on pain medication?'

'And anti-inflammatories. The leg has improved a lot. It's been nineteen months. I'm off the painkillers for the most part. I'll take them occasionally and the anti-inflammatories too if I have a big day of movement coming up.'

'I didn't know you were off the painkillers,' said Trig.

'Not completely. But on a good day I can get by without. Doctor, what about the sex with my husband? Am I cleared to do that? Because we're on our honeymoon.'

'Ah.' The doctor slid Trig a sideways glance. 'Again, if you're sensible and don't indulge in anything too rigorous you should be fine.'

Lena beamed. Trig frowned.

For a man on his honeymoon he didn't look altogether pleased about the lifting of the no-sex ban.

'You want us on the next flight home, don't you?' Lena accused as they left the doctor's rooms.

'The thought had crossed my mind.'

'Why?'

'Because your memory's still impaired.'

'It's not that impaired.'

'That's one opinion.'

'Aren't we meant to be meeting up with Jared while we're here? When's that scheduled for?'

'It's not. I haven't heard from him.' Trig nodded towards a dark grey saloon that was fast approaching. 'There's our driver.' The vehicle slid to a halt and Trig opened the rear door for her. Traffic backed up behind the vehicle but both Trig and the driver seemed unconcerned. 'I'm tossing up whether we should go to Bodrum or not,' Trig said as they got under way.

'Bodrum is indeed a most pleasant holiday destination,' offered the taxi driver. The driver's name was Yasar. Yasar was a cheerful man with many relatives.

'I promise to rest,' Lena said. Hopefully this would reassure him.

'And do exactly what I say,' Trig said.

'Was that in our marriage vows? I don't think it was.'

Trig sighed. 'You could at least pretend obedience. How else am I going to pretend that taking you to Bodrum is even a halfway good idea? Because it's not. It's the worst idea I've ever had, with the exception of one or two others.'

'What were the others?'

'Imbecilic.'

Lena grinned at him. 'I'd like to go to Bodrum. It sounds relaxing. I'll stay out of your way if there's work there for you that you want to chase up. I'm okay with you multitasking. We could fly there this afternoon after we shop.'

'Shop for what?'

'Clothes.' Lena leaned forward towards the driver. 'Yasar, are there any big department stores nearby?'

'Indeed, there are,' Yasar offered in a voice filled with deep despair. 'Although why anyone would want to shop there, when for marginally more effort I can take you to any number of specialty stores that also offer discretionary discounting—'

'Not today, Yasar,' Trig cut in firmly. 'Just find us a department store.'

Ten minutes later, Yasar slowed the car to a halt in front of a huge department store.

'How long are we going to be?' Trig asked her.

'Half an hour.'

'Half an hour,' said Yasar, looking to Trig. 'I shall be back in this very spot at exactly ten fifty. Shall I be bearing kebabs and cold beverages for you and your lady wife?'

'Yes,' said Trig. 'Yasar, what are you like at booking flights?'

'I have a gift for it,' said Yasar. 'I also have a cousin who is a travel agent.'

'See if your cousin can book us on a flight to Bodrum later this afternoon.'

Yasar nodded sagely.

'Handy guy,' she murmured as Yasar drove away.

'He's a fixer.'

They entered the store and headed past the perfume counters and towards the escalators, where a giant sign told them what items would be on what floor. 'I propose we divide and conquer,' she told him briskly. 'Second floor for you.'

'Second floor is women's evening wear.'

'Exactly. I need a dress to go dancing in. Don't bring too much sexy back and I don't do baby pink or ruffles.'

'But you could.'

'Yes, and you could do purple spandex but I don't buy it for you.'

'Good point. Where are you going while I'm on level two?'

'Level four.' She smiled angelically. 'Lingerie and nightwear.'

Trig peeled off onto the second floor of the department store with fear in his heart and lust in his soul. When Lena wanted something she had a frightening habit of getting it. Lena was buying lingerie and he'd been sent off to buy her a dress. If Trig wasn't mistaken, she was gearing up for the full wedding night experience.

With him.

A shop assistant hovered; one with Bambi eyes and more curves than a roller coaster. She looked him up and down, her eyes approving until she saw the wedding ring on his finger and then they turned assessing. 'May I assist you?' she said.

'I need a gown for my wife. She wants to go dancing.'

Twenty-five minutes later, he and Lena met at the

entrance doors to the store. Yasar and his taxi stood waiting, two take-away coffee cups in hand. Lena had a wide and wicked smile on her face and carried three shopping bags.

Trig had one bag and a headache.

'Yasar, did you know that this is our honeymoon?' said Lena when she got back into the taxi and accepted the hot tea and kebab that the driver handed her.

'But, *no*.'

'Yes, and I don't know anything about Bodrum but I do know that I want to stay somewhere magical and luxurious tonight. Somewhere with billowing gauze curtains and velvet pillows. A truly grand establishment where bite-sized delicacies are delivered to the room on a silver platter. It could even be a bridal suite in a fancy hotel.'

Trig stifled a groan. This was going nowhere good.

'Lady wife of Gentleman Sinclair, I do know of such a place in Bodrum. It is quite famous.'

'I have a credit card,' said Lena.

'Payment at this most exquisite abode may *only* be made by credit card,' said Yasar. 'Indeed, it is not for the financially challenged. I myself have never been there.' Yasar met Trig's gaze in the rear-view mirror. 'There are other options.'

Trig was all for exploring other options.

'What's it called?' Lena asked.

'Saul's Caravan. Though it is not a caravan, you understand. It is an old stone residence overlooking the city. It is thought to have once housed a King's concubine.'

'Do we have anywhere booked?' Lena turned to him, her eyes imploring.

'No. But...'

'But what?'

'I think I have a headache. I could be coming down with something. I'm probably not going to be of much use to you tonight, romance-wise, that's all. We could save ourselves for another time.'

Lena eyed him thoughtfully before turning her attention to Yasar. 'Yasar, what do you have for headaches?'

'There is a drink,' began Yasar, above the wailing of the radio.

Of course there was.

Lena went ahead and organised a two-night stay at Saul's Caravan. The hotel accommodation to date had been fine but nothing special, and her encounter with the pickpockets and subsequent visits to the doctor had left her feeling as if they needed some place special in order to get this honeymoon back on track.

A driver from Saul's Caravan collected them from the airport, his immaculate dark grey suit and the brand-new Mercedes he led them to an indication of what they might expect. The hotel stood high on a cliff face, grim, grey and surrounded by high stone walls half smothered in jasmine.

'Look.' Lena leaned across Trig to get a better look

as they passed the entry gates. 'It has a turret. I've always wanted a turret.'

'I've always wanted a puppy,' said Trig, but he smiled as they came to a stop at the hotel entrance.

The carved double entrance doors could have graced the Versailles palace. The mosaic tiles that covered the ground looked as if they belonged in a museum. A staggeringly beautiful woman greeted them and introduced herself as Aylin, the proprietor of Saul's Caravan. She didn't bother with check-in, but led them to their suite and showed them inside.

It felt a lot like stepping into Aladdin's cave. Silver candlesticks and burnished pewter ware glowed atop burnished wooden dressers and sideboards. Gauze drapes hung from the roof above the huge four-poster bed and there was enough exquisite linen draping the bed itself to open a linen store. Old tapestries hung on the walls, half a dozen Persian carpets scattered the floor.

Because why have just one?

The suite had a tiny courtyard garden and sweeping views of Bodrum and the Aegean.

There was an outdoor eating area and a small indoor sunken pool, half hidden behind a carved wooden partition. A life-sized marble lion stretched out next to the partition. He appeared to be protecting a sleeping cherub. A life-sized painted plaster Virgin Mary graced one corner of the room, a jade Buddha sat in the opposite corner, and a trompe l'oeil of what Lena suspected was a Muslim prayer covered an entire wall. The room also contained a harp, a pianola, fairy lights and a gong.

'Oh, yes,' murmured Lena.

'Are we still on the planet?' Trig clearly doubted it.

Lena headed for the en suite—which was not to be confused with the other bathing pool. 'Hey, Trig. There's a surfboard-shaped mirror right here in the dressing room, next to the Tinkerbell lamp. Do you feel at home yet? Tell me you do, because there are costumes here too—that or someone's left their clothes behind.' She reappeared. 'I love this place.'

'I think it's mental.'

'Yeah, but I'm not in my right mind now either and you won't be once I'm through with you. This place works on so many levels.'

Aylin smiled softly. 'This room is strategically lit of an evening,' she offered. 'There are lights, for example, beneath the bed.'

'Electrocution as well.' Trig nodded sagely. 'Tell me that doesn't cost extra.'

'It doesn't cost extra,' said Aylin.

Lena liked this woman already. 'See? What's not to love?'

Lena was on for the ride, the adventure, the unexpected.

'One night,' Trig said.

'I booked us in for two.'

'There's half a winged cherub sticking out of the ceiling.'

Lena looked up. Indeed there was. And it wasn't his

upper half. She chewed on her lip and stifled another smile. 'Definitely two.'

Trig rolled his eyes, but Lena knew she had him.

'Two nights,' she told Aylin sweetly and the woman nodded and stepped aside so that their driver could enter with their bags. A young woman followed in his wake, carrying a silver tray bearing refreshments. Another woman entered with a tray of fresh fruit.

'You feeling indulged enough yet, princess?' Trig wanted to know.

'Is the bed big enough for you?' she shot back. Because it was the biggest bed she'd ever seen. Antique. Custom made. Ever so slightly daunting. But Trig would fit on it and so would she.

'We're on our honeymoon,' Lena murmured and Aylin looked first at Lena and then at Trig in clear assessment of what he might bring to the honeymoon party. And smiled.

If there was ever a place for a scarred and insecure woman to seduce a man, this was it, decided Lena as the staff left and she started exploring her surroundings in earnest. The furniture choices and combinations had a whimsy about them—they celebrated the absurd and the unexpected, the ridiculous and the frayed. The blue and white tiled mosaic on the bathroom floor had a jagged crack running through one corner but still dared the viewer to gaze on it and call it anything but magnificent. You could find beauty in imperfection here. An imperfect woman might find courage here and the boldness to seduce a wary man.

Because her husband? Whatever else he was, he was also a wary man. Especially when it came to being physically intimate with her. Kisses, he delivered with impressive thoroughness and abandon. Hugs, touches and full body contact, he could do that too, provided everyone was wearing clothes.

Jump into bed and the man had a habit of leaving the room.

And maybe that had been on account of the doctor's orders, but Lena didn't entirely buy into that scenario.

Trig wasn't pushing the physical intimacy at all.

Take now, for example. They had everything they could possibly need when it came to an afternoon of seduction. They had water and wine, a tray full of finger-food delicacies and even a little hookah with a selection of flavoured tobaccos. And he stood there as if uncomfortable in his own skin, hunching slightly as he looked towards Bodrum with a brooding expression on his face.

He'd been brooding ever since he'd checked his phone—correction, one of his phones, because he had at least two that she'd seen.

He held it in his hand now, big thumb stroking absently over the screen. Whatever his mind was on, it wasn't on her.

And Lena did most firmly want it on her.

She came to stand beside him, freshly showered and wrapped in an emerald silk robe that she'd found hanging on the back of the bathroom door. 'That a work phone?'

'No. It's one of Damon's. His are less traceable than the ones from work.'

'There's a disturbing thought,' she said dryly.

'Yeah.' He finally turned to look at her and his expression turned even more brooding. 'Not that I have any objection to what you're wearing but what happened to your clothes?'

'They're coming up. You might have wanted me to take them back off.' There was that hunted look again. 'Guess not.'

'Well, not *immediately*. I figured you might like to try the food first. And the wine.' He headed for the table and put it between them. 'Champagne?' The champagne cork popped and Trig poured bubbly yellow liquid into delicate crystal flutes engraved with grape leaves and clusters. He poured himself one and drained it in one swift swallow.

Lena sipped at hers. 'I've never seen anyone do champagne flute shots before.'

'First time for everything,' he murmured, looking anywhere but at her. 'And I need to shower now. Right now. A lot. Really not clean.' He nodded far too enthusiastically and disappeared back inside.

Lena watched him go and sighed. Cleanliness was indeed a virtue, but still...

She found the shopping bag with the dress Trig had chosen for her and peeked inside. She put her hand in and pulled out a mass of cobalt-blue chiffon.

The dress had a fitted strapless bodice and layers of gauzy skirt that flared out gently from the waist and ended in a mass of ruffles.

'Do I do ruffles?' she murmured. "I don't recall that I do.'

She ditched the robe, slipped into the lilac strapless bra and matching panties that she'd bought earlier, and then slipped the dress over her head. The bodice fitted neatly once she'd found the zip. The skirt fell in soft waves to mid-calf and she grabbed onto a bedpost and swooshed her leg up through the layers, pointed toe and all. It was an altogether feminine creation and gloriously light and soft against her skin.

She *did* do ruffles.

But she'd forgotten to ask for shoes.

Never mind; they didn't *have* to go out dancing tonight. Nothing wrong with dancing barefoot here.

Her body felt good—as good as it was going to get. She reached for her make-up bag and painted her face in a tiny mirror pinned to the wall above three flying plaster ducks. Crowded, this room full of curiosities.

If her husband ran out of things to do to her and wanted to go exploring, he could always start opening drawers. He'd probably fall down a rabbit hole.

Twenty minutes later, Lena had done all the primping she could think of to do and her husband *still* hadn't emerged from the bathroom. Lena pounded on the door. 'Adrian, honey. You'd better not be in there taking the edge off. I have plans for that.'

Trig groaned.

'Really not reassuring,' she offered next. 'Is anything wrong?'

'Lena, I know what you want.' He had a great voice and he knew just how to drop it an octave and make it all husky and awkward. 'I just don't know that I can deliver the magical wedding-night experience you're after.'

Lena leaned her shoulder against the door and her hip soon followed. 'Why not?'

'Performance pressure,' came the husky reply.

'Seriously? You? I mean—you're the biggest showoff I know and you're not exactly inexperienced.' Or underendowed. She looked down at her rings and damned if they didn't start blurring on account of unshed tears. 'Didn't see that coming.'

Trig said nothing.

'If it helps any, I'm hardly Little Miss Confident when it comes to that area of our relationship,' she offered haltingly. 'I have body parts that aren't all that flexible any more. Not sure how that works when you get thrown into the mix. I mean... It *does* work between us, doesn't it? Sexually? *You* know this, even if I don't?'

'Yeah.' Inside the bathroom Trig stared at his reflection in the mirror and prayed for mercy. 'Works fine.'

What the hell else could he say? Tell her he had no idea and let her worry about that too?

'So, are you nearly done in there?'

'Yeah.' He'd been staring blankly at the mosaic on the floor for the last ten minutes, with the water beating down on his back and no idea how he was going to get through this night. 'I'll be out in a minute, and there'll be dancing and, y'know, amazing conversation and food and stuff. But not bed stuff. Not yet. I want to woo you first.' Woo? *Woo?* Who in this day and age said woo? He was losing his mind.

'You want another champagne?' she asked.

'That'd be good.' Maybe he could drink his way out of this. Or drink Lena under the table. No sex after that, just hangovers from hell and a Lena who'd *know* he'd sabotaged the evening deliberately. That was assuming that he could get Lena to drink heavily in the first place.

Bad idea. 'Actually, I don't want another drink right now. Maybe later.'

He heard her sigh, clear through the door.

He could always say he'd come down with a contagious social disease. Trig shuddered and thunked his head gently against the mirror. Not sure he really wanted to explore that one.

An argument, then. A rip-roaring quarrel that ended with Lena relegating him to the doghouse. He and Lena had argument down to a fine art. There'd be muscle memory, and synapse memory and maybe she'd *regain* her memory and then it'd really be on.

But he didn't want to argue with her either.

'We should go out tonight,' he said. 'We should go out right now and see the sights. You could seduce me while we're doing that. Or you could, y'know, get interested in the sights and leave the seduction for later.

We could dine out, go dancing. Make it like a date. I bet you don't remember any of our dates.'

Mainly because they'd never been on one.

'I remember the first time you took me kite surfing,' she offered.

'It doesn't count if your brother was there. Bodrum has a castle. They turned it into a maritime museum. Don't you want to go and see the castle? I bet it has turrets.' Lena liked turrets.

'Would it make you lose the performance anxiety?'

'Couldn't hurt. It'd also help if you didn't *mention* the performance anxiety.'

'Oh,' she said. 'Got it. So...sightseeing and then a dinner date?'

'Yes.' Maybe he could tire her out completely. Now there was a thought.

'Should I wear my dress?'

'Not for the sightseeing part.'

'So, we're coming back here before we go for dinner?'

'Not sure.'

'I'm taking that as a yes. We could have dinner here if we didn't feel like going out again.'

Or not. He could arrange it so that they didn't come back here. Avoiding that would mean avoiding the problem of Lena's near nakedness while she got changed, not to mention the wearing of that frothy blue dress the saleswoman had persuaded him to buy this morning.

Lena in that dress in this place was just courting

trouble. He eyed his reflection in the mirror and took a deep breath. 'I'll be out in a minute. And then we'll go.'

'There's no hurry.' She sounded a little bit wistful. 'I still have to get changed.'

So it took her husband half an hour to shower, shave and throw on a T-shirt and a pair of faded jeans. So she'd changed out of the pretty blue dress and thrown on a pair of grey shorts and another one of those simple cotton T-shirts that her suitcase seemed to be full of, and then she'd helped herself to more nibbles and poured herself another champagne by the time he appeared.

Adrian Sinclair was worth the wait.

Lena watched from the hanging love seat in the courtyard garden as he padded through the room, his bare feet making no sound as he stepped out onto the tiles. She knew those feet, from surfboards of old, and she knew those big hands for she'd grasped them often enough as he'd reached down to haul her into a boat or up a cliff face. She knew what his hair looked like wet because she'd seen it wet a thousand times. She knew this man and loved him. And she knew he loved her.

He didn't need to have performance anxiety. Not around her. She honestly had no idea why he would.

'Ready to go?' he asked, and she nodded.

'We have a driver,' she told him. 'He'll drop us off and pick us up wherever we want.'

Trig nodded.

'Did you know that this place is still family-owned? About fifty years ago, the upkeep was sending the family broke and a terrace wall fell down, fortunately not on any guests, but they did find an iron strongbox buried in the footings. It was full of jewellery.'

'Jewellery fit for a princess?'

'Better.' Lena grinned. 'Jewels designed to placate a royal concubine. They sold three pieces, kept the rest, and it was enough to fully restore this place and run it as a luxury hotel until the hotel became profitable in its own right. Did you know that there are only ten guests here at any one time and eighteen permanent staff?'

'I do now.'

'And that they'll shop for us if we tell them what we want?'

'What do you want?'

'Shoes. To go with the dress you bought me earlier. Which is glorious, by the way. I tried it on.'

'Does it fit?'

'To perfection.'

'Not sure I got the colour right.'

'I love it. It makes me feel like a dancer and I almost have curves.' She'd never had curves. 'Do you remember that dress you, Jared and Poppy helped me pick out when I was in year twelve?'

In the absence of a mother's guidance, Lena had done her best with buying things like make-up and clothes, but the sheer choice that her father's bankcard had provided had always overwhelmed her, and when it had come to choosing a dress for the school formal, Jared and Trig had just kept saying no. No to the little black dress because she didn't have enough curves to pull it off. No to the A-line silk tunic with the psychedelic purple swirls because it was far too short and altogether too easy for someone to get their hands beneath it. And she'd been adamantly against any of the more feminine creations Poppy had urged her towards. Hard to embrace feminine clothing when she'd been so set on being one of the boys. She'd finally settled on a glittery red flapper creation with enough crystal beading hanging off it to sink a boat. 'That dress was so wrong.'

'That dress did not get my vote,' said Trig as he slipped on a pair of shoes and pocketed his wallet. 'It looked like a lampshade and weighed a ton. You could have worn it as a weight belt while diving.'

He did remember it. 'Did I ever tell you that when I danced in it the beaded fringe flew out and started smacking people?'

'Maybe you were dancing too close to them.'

'Nope. Those fringes were really long. People got whacked from half a metre away. I didn't get up close and personal with anyone at that dance.'

'Probably because of the dress.'

'Pretty sure it was because of me.' Lena smoothed her fingers down the front of her serviceable shorts. 'No date. No dance partners other than whoever was dancing in the group.' Lena *knew* she pursued things too aggressively at times. Sports, adrenaline highs, men…boy, could she scare men away when she wanted to. And Trig and Jared had encouraged it.

Maybe she *had* been too focused on sex these past few days.

Maybe she needed to cut her husband a break.

'I remember wanting to ask you to be my partner for that night,' she said. 'It would have made it bearable.'

'Why didn't you?'

'You were twelve hundred kilometres away. And Jared said you were busy.'

'Not that busy,' her husband said, after a pause. 'I also wasn't sure whether I wanted to mess with the status quo between you, me and Jared. I didn't want you to get the wrong idea—or possibly the same ideas that I had. You and Jared were my friendship group, my safety net, and I didn't fit anywhere else. If I stuffed that up I'd have no one.'

Trig had his hands in his pockets and a frown on his face but he nodded as if he understood. 'Weigh your risks.'

'Exactly.'

He nodded again, his eyes dark with some unidentifiable emotion. 'So about this date. You ready to go?'

She most certainly was.

Trig had more than one ulterior motive for having the driver drop them at the marina rather than the castle. This was the marina that Amos Carter had steered them towards. Jericho3 could be the name of a boat. It sounded too easy, but Trig didn't mind easy. Right now he craved it. His other reason was nastier, because it involved making Lena walk to the castle from the marina—a distance she could have covered with ease two years ago, but this was now and he knew that she'd have trouble even making it to the castle from here, no matter how often she stopped for a breather along the way.

'Are we looking for anything in particular?' Lena asked, with her gaze firmly fixed on the half a dozen sturdy wooden tourist yachts bobbing up and down in their moorings. The sterns of the boats were loaded with cushions and lounges. The undercover bow areas contained dining tables and chairs. The boats were manned by young men with flashing white smiles and darkly suntanned skin. 'Jericho3 perhaps?'

'Yes.'

'I *knew* it.' Lena slid her hand in the crook of his elbow. 'I knew you had an ulterior motive for dragging us down here this afternoon. You think it's the name of a boat?'

'No harm in looking.' Trig eyed the people on the nearby tourist yachts.

'No women,' said Lena.

'Maybe they're below.'

'Maybe we could do a trip on one of them. Good way to look around, make some enquiries.'

'You don't want to go out on those boats.' The girl who sidled up to them had a bright smile, copper-coloured hair and enough confidence for a dozen street touts. 'Come back tomorrow morning before ten if you want a day tour.'

'Maybe we want a night tour,' said Lena.

'You might,' said the girl. 'But not on those boats. See all the pretty boys? You pay them and they serve you. The bedrooms are below. Sometimes they don't even bother with bedrooms. These are the night *pleasure* boats.'

'Oh.' Lena coloured.

Trig grinned. 'We're not interested.'

'I know,' said the girl. 'You want *my* boat. Taxi service only. Take you around the castle and then on a tour of the bay. Drop you back here or at the castle marina if you'd rather. Twenty-five lira.'

'Seems a little steep,' said Trig.

'I also saved you from the night boats.'

'What if we *had* wanted the night boats?' Trig asked curiously.

'Then I would have recommended my friend Akbar's fine vessel. It is the most orderly of all the pleasure yachts because he does not allow drug taking or unruly behaviour on board. Nor does he drug your drinks and steal all your money, unlike some.'

'What a gentleman,' said Lena. 'And your taxi is where?'

'Down here.'

The girl's water taxi was in fact a decent-sized cruiser. 'I have lifejackets,' she told them as she hopped nimbly into it, grabbed at a rope and started manoeuvring the cruiser towards a nearby ladder, attached to the wharf. 'My pilot's licence is legitimate. Twenty lira, because I like you. And I'll tell you stories about Bodrum night life along the way.'

Lena glanced at Trig. 'Means I don't have to walk to the castle. I'm good with this.'

'How are you going to get into the boat?'

'Slowly. Possibly with your help. As in you go first and then when I look like I'm going to fall, you catch me. It's all part of my asking-for-help-if-I-need-it plan. You like this plan, I hasten to add.'

'How do you know?'

'Because you said so.'

'You remember that?'

Lena frowned. 'Not as a specific memory. More of a general knowledge thing. Why? Am I wrong? Are you on a quest to make me more independent?'

'No.' The girl bumped the boat against the ladder. Trig climbed down and drew Lena down after him, hands to her waist as he lifted her from the ladder into the cruiser. 'You want help, I'm your man.'

'Nice,' said the girl approvingly, and winked at Lena. 'What'd you do to your leg?'

'Stuffed it,' Lena said. 'And the hip. And parts of the spine.'

The girl started the motor. 'You should sit. I'll go slow. Even when I'm out of the marina.'

'Do me a favour, and don't,' said Lena, coming to stand by the girl. 'I'm thinking of buying a speedboat. I want to feel how my body holds up to a bit of speed.'

'You got it,' said the girl, and when they cleared

the marina and turned towards Bodrum castle she gunned it. Lena stood beside her, one hand on the back of the pilot's seat and the other on the top of the windscreen.

She wasn't even *trying* to seduce him, decided Trig darkly. She was simply being her old self—the one who saw opportunity at every turn and seized it. The one who only had to look at him and smile in order to seduce him.

She was looking back at him now, her hair whipping across her face. That smile. That one right there.

'I can do this,' she said.

'See how you pull up tomorrow.'

Her eyes dimmed but her chin came up and he loved that about her too. Never tell Lena she couldn't do something, because she'd do it just to prove you wrong.

'This is the castle,' said the girl over the roar of the engines. 'It was built by the Knights Hospitaller, otherwise known as The Knights of the Order of St John. They called it St Peter's Castle and it served as a refuge and stronghold for all the Christians in the land and beyond. Later, the castle was surrendered to Sultan Suleiman and became a mosque. *That* got destroyed by the French in World War One, and then it became a museum. Take a tour. Very special.'

'What about the things you don't learn on castle tours?' Trig asked. 'There's a lot of money floating in this bay. Where does it all come from?'

The girl shot him a sharp glance. Trig did his best to look harmless.

'Tourists,' she said finally. 'Hedonists. The pleasure seekers of Eastern Europe. You can indulge in anything here, for a price. Many people come to do just that.'

'Is the crime organised?'

'Very.'

'Who are the main players?'

'Turks. Russians.'

'Any Asians?'

'No.'

'Ever heard of a boat called the *Jericho3*?'

'I got no business with anyone connected to the *Jericho3*,' their copper-haired pilot offered grimly. 'I like to keep it that way.'

'Know where we can find it?'

'No.'

'Wouldn't be asking if I didn't need to know.'

'I can't help you, man. Little matter of staying alive.'

'No problem.' Trig smiled easily. Harmless. See? 'Tell us about the night life. Tourist stuff only.'

The girl told them about open-air night clubs that backed onto the sea. She told them about the live music and the bars, the street parties and light shows. She dropped them off at the wharf below the castle's eastern walls and Trig paid her and tipped well, and told her she didn't need to take them any further and her sunny smile reappeared.

'You had me worried, big guy.'

'Don't be.'

Her eyes narrowed. 'That vessel you mentioned. How much do you know about it?'

'I have a name. I have a friend who might be on it.'

'By choice?'

Trig shrugged.

The girl shook her head. 'It's a mega yacht, with helicopters, a defence system, and a seventy-strong crew, most of them Russian. Thirty or so guest rooms. Not everyone's a guest.'

'I don't see anything like that here.'

'It stays offshore. Nice and private out there.'

'How does it refuel?'

'Tanker.'

'Anyone ever come in off it?'

'A woman and a kid. They go to the hospital here once a week, regular as clockwork.'

'Which day?'

'Tomorrow. Look for a power cruiser coming in to this wharf around ten a.m.'

'Thanks.'

'You seem nice,' she said. 'Don't be a dead man.' And then she got under way.

'Guess that saves us walking past a thousand small sailing yachts,' said Lena. 'Really wasn't looking forward to that.'

Trig snorted. 'I can't believe you just admitted that.'

'What? That walking more than a mile or so wears me out?'

'Yes.'

'It's hardly a secret.'

'I know. But you usually don't like admitting it.'

'I'm older and wiser now. I also don't mind admitting complete ignorance as to why we're here. You do realise that I can't remember *anything* about why that yacht is so important? Or who you think might be on it.'

'I realise.'

'Care to share?'

'Not really. Honeymoon, remember?'

'I do remember.' Lena stared up at the towering castle. 'That is a big castle.'

'I know. The view from the top of that turret is going to be *great*.'

'Maybe if I had a *week*,' she joked dryly. 'I used to have a healthy relationship with steps. Now they just send me weak in the knees.'

'I'll carry you,' he heard himself suggest.

'That'll wear *you* out,' she said. 'Let's just see a bit of the museum.'

They managed to get through half of one wing of the museum before closing time. They took it easy and avoided steps.

And Lena wore herself out anyway.

'Aches don't count if you had fun getting them,' she told him as they waited for their ride back to the hotel. 'It also makes relaxing at the end of the day *so good*. Please tell me it's the end of the day.'

'There's still dinner and dancing to go.'

'Oh.' Lena visibly wilted. 'Right.'

'Aches don't count if you have fun getting them.' Trig grinned. Lena thumped him and for a split second all was well with his world.

The sun had slid low in the sky by the time they arrived back at the hotel. Lena had stiffened up during the drive and Trig watched her take her time getting out of the car. He didn't miss a wince. Neither did the driver.

'We have a heated bathing pool that is very relaxing,' the driver told them as he escorted them to the front of the house.

'You mean the one in the room?' asked Lena.

'In addition to the one in the room.'

'I love Turkey,' murmured Lena.

'Also an in-house masseuse.'

'Perfect. What's the dress code for this bathing pool?'

'Swimwear is, of course, required. But the bathing caps need not be worn. The hair need not need be covered.'

'That's a requirement in some places?'

'In some places it is so. For cultural reasons, you understand. The bathing in such establishments is also segregated. But not here.' The driver glanced at Trig. 'Shall I arrange beverages for two out by the pool?'

'Not for me. I have some calls to make,' said Trig. 'But Lena might like something.'

'What would you suggest?' Lena asked the driver.

'For the thirsty I might suggest susurluk ayrani. It

is a chilled drink made from yoghurt and garnished with mint. Very refreshing.'

'I would like to feel refreshed,' said Lena.

'You want me to bring your swimmers out to the pool?' Trig had guilt now. Lots and lots of guilt on account of all the walking he'd encouraged Lena to do today.

'No, I'll change in the room. I want to do it in front of the mirror next to the Tinkerbell lamp, just in case the mirror tells me I'm the fairest of them all.'

'I wouldn't discount it.'

'And I wouldn't want to miss it. You don't mind me taking a dip and leaving you to your own devices for a while?' she asked.

'Not at all. Take your time. Relax.'

'You know what would make that sentence perfect? If you added, "I'll order dinner for us and I'll get them to set it up in our little courtyard garden."'

'You don't want to go back into Bodrum?'

'I *really* don't want to go back into Bodrum. We could dine and dance here. You could put me straight to bed when I fall asleep with my head on your shoulder, having mistaken you for a gently swaying mountain.'

'Tempting.'

'I knew you'd see it my way.'

'Go and bathe. I'll have a menu sent to you out by the pool. You do realise that I'm indulging you completely?'

'You're a good man.'

'I'll see what the mirror says.' He was pretty sure the mirror would call him a fool.

Lena headed towards the suite. Trig headed back out through those massive entrance doors and decided to investigate the hotel perimeter. He was nosey that way, and he needed privacy in order to make a call.

He pulled out Damon's phone and checked for messages. From Jared. From Damon. From anyone.

Nothing.

He put a call through to Damon next.

'I'm in Bodrum in a concubine's lair overlooking the castle of St Peter,' he said, when Damon picked up.

'Amen,' said Damon.

'That all you got?'

'I can always put Ruby on. She might have more.'

'Do that.'

'No. How's Lena?'

'She still thinks we're on our honeymoon.'

'Then why aren't you on a plane?'

'Because I'm following a lead on Jared. There's a mega yacht hereabouts called the *Jericho3*. I need to know more about it. Ownership. Specs. Whatever you can find within the next eight hours.'

'You thinking of paying it a visit?'

'No. I'm thinking that would be suicide. My best hope is that Jared's worked his way onto it. Worst-case scenario—he's a prisoner on it.'

'How are you going to find out which?'

'Hopefully, Jared's going to show himself.'

'Assuming he can.'

'Yeah,' muttered Trig. 'Let's assume that for now.'

'Are you letting Lena in on any of this?'

'I'm about to.'

'Is that wise? She's not exactly operational.'

'I can protect her. She's only after a glimpse of Jared. Proof that he's alive. We'll keep our distance.'

'Does she *remember* wanting to see him?'

'She will. And when she does, she'll have already seen him and won't feel inclined to go tearing after Jared again. Or would you rather I brought her home and we end up back here in another week's time doing exactly the same thing?'

Damon sighed.

'It's under control. I'll bring her home as soon as she's seen Jared. How soon can you and Ruby get to the beach house?'

'About that. Are you sure you're going to need us there?'

'Your sister thinks I married her. You want me to repeat that?'

'No, I got it.' Damon's voice was droll, very droll.

'I would love to marry Lena, I would. But I haven't married her yet and she is going to have my balls when she finds out. She's going to need someone to scream at. That would be me. Then she's going to need someone to argue with some more, once she's calmed down. That would be you. And then someone needs to argue my case. That's where Ruby comes in.'

'Does Ruby know that she's arguing your case?'

'Not yet. Put her on.'

'No can do. Ruby's asleep and I'm not waking her up. She's sleeping for three.'

'What?'

'Twins.'

'God help us.'

'Your congratulations are most heartily accepted.'

'Congratulations,' Trig said quickly. 'I mean…yeah. Congratulations. Twice.'

Did it make him a bad person that his first thought was not for Ruby and Damon's happiness but that he was never going to have that? That Lena was never going to know babies the way Ruby would know them. 'Is everything okay? With Ruby and the babies?'

'Everything's good. There's no real reason Ruby can't travel. I'm just…'

'I get it.' He got it.

'Lena can come to Hong Kong. You can both come, and we'll do the not-exactly-married debrief here.'

'Sold.' What else could he say? The only reason he'd chosen Damon's beach house as the debrief venue in the first place was because Lena had spent so much time there and the surroundings would be familiar. They could work around that. Lena's father lived in Hong Kong. He had a penthouse there. Maybe that would count as home ground too.

'Better get you that information,' Damon said. 'Stay safe.' And then he was gone.

Trig scrolled through the pictures he'd taken of the castle and picked one that he'd taken from the wharf.

He sent it to Jared's number. He didn't add words, but he thought them.

We're here, man. And if we can't get to you you're going to have to come to us.

If you can.

NINE

—

The meal Lena ordered for them turned out to be a feast. Saul's Caravan set a lavish table, and not just in terms of the food. Lena discovered that fine china did not have to match when each piece was exquisite. She discovered that solid silver water pitchers and solid silver serving trays were mighty heavy, and that meze dishes were only the precursor to the main meal and that maybe she shouldn't have tried a little bit of everything, because when the spicy lamb dish arrived, Lena had barely any room left in her stomach.

'How much did you order?' Trig had partaken heartily of the meze too.

'I ordered the traditional feast for two, and Aylin mentioned something about five courses.' They'd started with dips and bread and then moved on to the meze. 'I'm thinking we're up to course three and I'm pretty sure the last course involves coffee.'

Lena served a small portion of the lamb onto her

heavily patterned blue and white plate and avoided the rice altogether. She indicated that she would serve Trig too, and he held out his plate while she spooned lamb onto it. 'Enough?'

'Thanks.'

He'd been on his best gentlemanly behaviour all evening. Keeping her wine glass topped up, saying he liked the dress and ignoring the fact that she wasn't wearing any shoes and that her hair was still half damp from her swim and the shower she'd taken afterwards.

She'd made some effort—she had make-up and perfume on. Trig had made an effort too, for he'd dug a white collared shirt out of his bag and had it ironed before putting it on over jeans.

He'd never blended into the background easily, Trig Sinclair. His size had always made people look twice and the reckless glint in his eyes had usually kept their attention. Put him and Jared together, turn them loose on a party or a bar and chaos ensued. Women wanted to bed them, men wanted to challenge them and Lena often wanted to knock their heads together and tell them to grow up.

Looking at Trig tonight, his face smiling but his eyes guarded, Lena thought that maybe he *had* grown up. And that Lena had somehow missed it.

'Five things you never wanted to be,' she said. It was an old game, this one. A way of filling in conversation and acquiring information that you might not already know.

'Conflicted,' he said.

'About what?'

'You. Your past and my part in it. I always assumed that by letting you tag along with us whenever we went windsurfing or hang-gliding or whatever fool adrenaline rush we were on that week, that Jared and I were giving you options. It never occurred to me that we were limiting them. You followed us into covert operations without even thinking about the consequences. None of us did, but you're the one who got busted up. That weighs on me a lot.'

'Where's this coming from?'

'I spoke to Damon earlier. We talked about you. About your limitations.'

'Thanks for nothing.'

'Ruby's pregnant.'

'Oh.' She refused to feel envy. She refused to feel longing. Those emotions had no place in the presence of Ruby's good news. 'That's good, isn't it? I get to be an auntie. Ruby gets to buy headbands for a baby. You can't tell me you're not looking forward to that.'

Trig's eyes warmed ever so slightly. 'Maybe. And it's babies. Plural. She's having twins.'

'Seriously?' Lena laughed. 'That is awesome. You think they'd let us borrow them?'

'I want children, Lena.'

Lena's laughter stuck in her throat. They hadn't talked about this; she knew it instinctively. Why hadn't they ever talked about this?

'No can do. I do know my limitations in that regard. You'll get no biological children from me.'

'We could adopt,' her husband said gruffly.

'We could.' That was one option. 'Or you could have a biological child with someone else. We could explore surrogacy.'

'You'd consider that?'

'You might have to get me a good shrink, but, yes. I could get on board with that. Could you?'

'I'd probably have to share your shrink for a while.'

'I could probably be your shrink for a while. These past couple of years I've become intimately acquainted with helplessness, hopelessness, anger, envy and old-fashioned irrational behaviour. I can show you round.'

Trig smiled at that and she reached forward and covered his hand with her own. 'Don't give up on me.'

'Never.'

This was why she'd married this man.

'I feel as if I'm in a place where I don't have to run to keep up any more,' she confessed. 'I *can't* run any more. Best I can do is hold my ground and stumble along, and you know what? You're still there for me, and my family is still there, because it was never about me keeping up. It was about me believing that I belonged and I *do* believe that now. I'm happy now. I married you, which I have to say is probably the smartest thing I've ever done.'

'About that...' His gaze flickered to the bed.

'Yes, about that. No pressure.'

'Right,' said Trig faintly and Lena smiled and cut him a break.

'How's your food?'

'Good.' Trig loaded up his fork and looked at it as if he couldn't quite remember where it should go.

Lena smiled and took a quick bite of the fragrant lamb stew. Tasty.

'Forget the bed,' she said, although she hadn't. 'We still have several more courses to get through, and dancing still to go. I have my dancing frock on and everything.'

'But no shoes.'

'I don't need shoes. You're not wearing any either,' she felt obliged to point out.

'There's no music.'

'I found some pianola rolls. I put one in. Want to see if it plays?'

'You love this room,' he said with a crooked smile as she rose from the table, caught hold of his hand and tugged him towards the pianola.

'I really do. It's a little bit beautiful, a whole lot fascinating, and kind of cracked when you look up close. I'm hoping it might be the way you see me. Because, newfound sense of belonging or not, I'm *still* trying to figure out what you see in me.'

She fiddled with the pianola settings and the machine began to play a bright and jazzy tune that put her in mind of Gershwin and New York.

'I should have packed the red lampshade dress.'

'Or you could sit this one out.'

'Good idea.' She reached for another of the scrolls crammed into the shelving beside the pianola. 'Hey, I remember this one from my mother's jewellery box! Open the lid and music played and the little ballerina went round and round and round.'

'I don't want to go round and round,' said Trig.

She pulled out another roll. 'ABBA?'

'Don't make me shoot you.'

'You do realise you're not going to be able to threaten our children or our nephews and nieces with a shotgun every time they don't share your taste?'

'I'll figure something out.'

'What about this one?' she said, holding up a pianola roll for his inspection. 'I think it's French.' It was also something she could sway to—her dancing skills hadn't exactly improved with age. 'Bear with me,' she said as she went to swap the rolls, only now Trig had decided to figure out how pianolas worked too. 'Focus.'

'I am focused.'

'On me.'

He poked his head back out of the old machine's innards. 'But I can focus on you any time.'

He looked sincere. He sounded sincere. He set the pianola roll to rolling and the first few notes of gentle piano music flowed into the room.

'Seems a little slow,' he murmured.

'It's perfect. Which carpet would you like to dance on?'

He smiled at that. 'The blue one by the end of the bed.'

'That's your favourite? Because I'm thinking of buying one just like it for the farmhouse on the banks of the lazy river.'

'I do like the idea of a farmhouse on the banks of a lazy river,' he admitted. Moments later he surrendered a wry smile and held out his hand for hers. When they reached the blue carpet he swung her gently around and into his arms and she put her hand to his chest, deeply satisfied when he drew a swift breath. His nipples had tightened and wasn't that a pretty sight against the cotton of his shirt? She swiped her thumb across one well-defined little bump and he bit back a whimper. 'You like that?'

He nodded.

She pressed a gentle kiss to his jaw next. 'And that?'

'Not complaining.'

'Not encouraging me either.'

'About that—'

She kissed his throat next and slid her hands beneath his shirt as he stood there and trembled beneath her touch. Heady business, seducing this husband of hers.

'We should dance,' he muttered.

'To do that I'm pretty sure someone has to move.'

So he stepped in closer, wrapped his hands around her waist and began to move. He'd always been athletic. Occasionally, in the midst of one of his teenage growth spurts, he'd get a little clumsy until he figured out the workings of his bigger, broader body.

He wasn't clumsy now.

Lena let her body follow where he led, and revelled in the brush of her chest against his, of her hips against his. Trig's eyes darkened as he pushed her hair back off her face with his fingertips.

'You do that a lot,' she murmured.

'Been wanting to do it for years.'

'What stopped you?'

'I wasn't sure if it was what you wanted. Still not sure.'

'I'm sure,' she said, but he was already turning away.

'C'mon, let's finish the feast,' he said and drew her back towards the table. They finished their main course and then smiling people cleared the table and dessert and coffee arrived.

Lena looked at the table laden with sweet delicacies and groaned. 'I can't.' There was simply no room left in her stomach.

Trig grinned and popped a baklava into his mouth.

'Oh, stuff it,' she said and reached for a baklava too.

Trig began to laugh, a sound that was front and centre of so many of her memories. He hadn't laughed much on this trip. For a man on his honeymoon he seemed to have a hell of a lot on his mind.

'Are you really worried about having sex with me?' she asked and Trig promptly swallowed down hard on his baklava. 'Because I truly don't understand why.'

'I just want you to have all your memories back first.'

'I don't understand that either. What's wrong with making new memories? I'm loving these new memories.'

Trig sat back and began to fiddle with the stem of his wine glass. 'Me too.'

'Is it the room? Is it too weird? Because, I have to say... I really like this place. I could get naked here and my scars wouldn't look that out of place amongst the freaky furnishings. They fit. I fit. Being here with you in this place, it's like a gift. Makes me want to check my inhibitions at the door.'

Trig pinned her with an intent gaze. 'What inhibitions?'

'Well, there's the scars... I saw the way people stared at me in the bath house. I know the marks aren't pretty, they're never going to be pretty but they're mine and the getting of them wasn't without honour. You told me that.'

'Lena—'

'We don't have to have the lights on. They can be off.'

'I thought you said you were checking your inhibitions at the door?'

'I'm just thinking about ways to make it better for you. You said you had performance pressure. I wondered if maybe you had trouble staying interested because of the scars.'

'I don't need the lights off,' he said flatly.

'Because you wouldn't have to touch them. The scars, I mean. I don't know what we usually do, but I do know that they wouldn't be a turn-on for you. You probably just...skim.'

'Lena, you have no idea what you're talking about,'

he said icily. 'I love you. Every contrary bit of you. Why the *hell* would I want to skim?'

He moved fast when he wanted to. He swept her off her feet and the next thing she knew she was on the bed and Trig was sinking down next to her, sending pillows tumbling to the floor. No weight on her at all but for the pressure of his hands curling around her wrists as he pinned her arms above her head.

'I don't skim,' he rasped, and dragged his lips from her temple to the edge of her mouth. 'Not with you. How the hell can you not know that?'

And then his lips were on hers and she opened for him and tasted champagne and cinnamon and the truth of his desire for her and it lit her blood faster than anything else ever could.

He didn't rush. He kissed her for a good long while before moving on to her shoulders and her throat. By the time his lips skated the bodice of her dress, Lena was writhing against him, impatient for more. He found the zipper on her dress and it slid down easy and then his lips were on her again, his tongue curling around her nipple, flicking over it and then sucking softly, testing to see which one she liked best and hands down the sucking won. Hands in his hair she told him that, with her head flung back and her breath gone ragged.

He began to edge her dress down further but she stopped him with her hands. 'Lights off,' she whispered.

'No.'

He shed his shirt, he got all the way undressed, not a shy bone in his body, and she loved that about him, even as she struggled with shedding her dress. He let her keep her panties on as he pressed open-mouthed kisses to the underside of her breasts and then her ribs and then his fingers touched the scar tissue that ran all the way from hip to groin. He pushed her legs apart and licked a stripe straight up the worst of the scars and she shuddered beneath the onslaught.

'Don't,' she whimpered. She didn't need this. He didn't need to do this.

But he pressed soft kisses into the rest of her scars next and then set his mouth to the centre of her panties and started drawing circles with his tongue. Ever smaller circles until she was pushing those panties down herself and the minute she had them off one leg he got one arm beneath her buttocks and set his mouth to her again.

She couldn't stop watching him and he kept his eyes on her, right up until his fingers joined the party and exposed her even more.

And then his lips were back on her scars and his cheek felt soft against them as he explored them with exactly the same attention as he'd given to the rest of her.

'You don't ever need to hide these from me,' he muttered, while his fingers continued to work their magic, rendering her slick and ready for him. 'I've seen them. I've watched you fight against them, get angry at them, despair of them but those are your emotions, not mine. These marks on your skin are a part of you now and I love them. I love you.'

He eased back up the bed until they were face-to-face again.

'Say it,' he demanded softly. 'Say, "Trig loves all of me and always will and I will never doubt it".'

'Trig loves me,' she whispered.

'Louder.'

'Trig loves me,' she said more firmly.

'Again.'

'You love me. Now would you mind *showing* me?'

'Been showing you for years.'

He eased onto his back, his gaze intent, willing her to follow, and she went with him, hands to his chest as she straddled him. Damn but he was built. She wasn't going to break him, that was for sure. She wondered how careful he had to be when it came to not breaking her.

'Take your time,' he muttered. 'There's no rush.'

'That's good.' Because she wasn't in any hurry.

She started at his shoulders, touching and tasting, not skimming as she moved down his torso and learned the way his muscles ran and bunched. She put her hand over his and learned the rhythms he liked, the little flick of his thumb at the top of each stroke, and eventually she wet her lips and took him in her mouth, just the tip and took his curse as a benediction.

His hand fell away and she took him in deeper, feeling the stretch in her lips because he was beautifully proportioned all over and wasn't exactly small. She tried to take a little more but ended up pulling off him with a loud pop. 'Damn but you'd think I'd remember that,' she offered. 'Not to mention what I used to do with it because right now I'm guessing that deep throating you is out unless I'm a hell of a lot more practised at this than I appear to be.'

Trig groaned and hooked his hands beneath her armpits and the next minute he was kissing her again and surging against her, not inside her, not yet, but doing a mighty fine job of jutting up against her sweet spot regardless.

He had a thing about her hair, winding his hands in it as he grasped her head and deepened the kiss. He had a thing for wrapping his arms around her, one hand between her shoulder blades and the other palming her buttocks. He had a thing about kisses, deep and dirty.

Finally, she sat up and took him in hand and positioned him at her entrance. He put his hands to her hips and bit his lower lip, his eyes a hot glitter as he gave a little push.

Lena gasped. Trig stopped, closed his eyes and breathed.

She pitched forward, skin against skin, as much as she could. 'Kiss me through it,' she whispered against his lips, and he did, until he was embedded all the way inside her.

'You okay?' he asked.

'I will be.'

'You sure?'

'You know me. I love a good challenge.'

'You're not exactly reassuring me here, Lena.'

'You don't need reassuring—we've done this before.' She moved, a slow slide, a little pitch from side to side. He controlled her with his hands at her waist, lifting until she was almost off him, before sliding slowly back into her.

This time they both groaned.

He kept the pace slow and the rhythm easy. 'You're holding back on me, aren't you?' she whispered. 'I thought you said you were all in?'

'I *am* all in. Which is why I'm holding back on you.'

The man had a point. 'Doesn't seem exactly fair.'

'I'm good,' he said. 'Any gooder and I'll be gone.'

'Still—'

'Why are you even thinking?' he said, and flipped her over and kissed her, probably just to shut her up, but the kiss turned sweet and tender somewhere along the way, and his hands were so very gentle as he slid between her legs and began to move.

She stopped thinking around about the time he tilted her hips just so and rocked against her. Every muscle in her stomach and below tightened in response.

'You like that?' he murmured against her lips.

'Just like that.'

So he gave it to her exactly like that and shot her up to a place where she didn't have to think at all.

Just feel.

* * *

Trig woke well before the dawn, pretending sleep, watching Lena sleep until he couldn't stay there a moment longer. Regret rode him hard and shame followed suit. He hadn't meant to lie beyond the hospital emergency rooms. He'd never meant to lie to Lena at all, but the lies had just kept coming and there'd never been a time to tell her straight that they weren't married.

Except maybe last night.

Or the one before that.

Rolling from the bed, he groped around on the floor for his sweat pants and pulled them on. He headed for the courtyard and some air, looking out over the low stone fence at the lights of the city below. A party city, some said. A reckless place where people left their inhibitions behind and went after what they truly wanted.

Last night he'd taken what he'd wanted and to hell with the consequences.

This morning he wouldn't be able to look at himself in the mirror.

He heard the rustle of bedcovers followed by a barely there groan. He turned and watched as Lena slipped from the bed and limped over to her suitcase. She drew out a white baby-doll nightie and slipped it on, lifting her hair out from underneath it. She tried to finger-comb her hair, caught him looking at her and stopped and shot him a rueful smile.

What was she thinking? What was her brain *doing* when it buried some memories and made a meal out of others? Why had she found it so easy to believe that they were married?

She walked up to his side and turned her back on the city lights in favour of leaning back against the wall and looking at him.

He couldn't hold her gaze.

He leaned forward, hands to the wall and kept his eyes on the city. He shouldn't have given in. Nobody was perfect, he knew that, but *hell*. His abuse of Lena's trust was staggering.

'Couldn't sleep?'

'No.'

'Anything to do with me?'

'No.'

'Pretty sure you're lying.'

'Yeah, well. I do that.'

Lena wrapped her arms around her waist as if cold. 'Why?'

Trig closed his eyes. 'Just one bad call leading to the next, I guess. I got no excuses for you, Lena.'

She stayed silent for a while after that and Trig willed her to go away, go back to bed, anywhere as long as it was away from him. But she didn't go anywhere, just ducked her head and bumped her shoulder against his. Wanting body contact, more body contact, and he flinched beneath the weight of her need and his guilt.

'What else have you lied about?' she asked raggedly.

Where did he even start?

'Do you love me?' she whispered and he closed his eyes and told her the one truth that had never wavered.

'So much.'

'Then it's the job you're lying about. You keep checking your phone. Something's up. Is it a job? For ASIS?'

'There is a job here,' he offered, and cursed himself for taking the coward's way out. 'And you do need to know the basics of it, because it involves Jared, and because before you got concussed you were spearheading it.'

Lena blinked and then put the heels of her hands to her eyes in a gesture he knew of old.

'I don't remember,' she whispered.

'I know.'

'Then isn't it time you told me why we're here?'

'We're here to find Jared.'

'And then what?'

'And then we leave.'

'Doesn't sound like much of a job.'

'Finding him's the catch.'

'*Jericho3*,' she murmured.

'I had Damon do some digging. The owner's a billionaire arms dealer. Russian.'

'Specialising in what?'

'Everything.'

'And that's where you think Jared is?'

'Best guess. Truth is, I don't know. He could be undercover. He might not want to break cover. He might not be able to break cover.'

'If Jared's undercover, why does he want to see us at all?'

'Didn't say he did. We're the ones pushing for contact.'

'But why?'

'The old you is concerned for Jared's safety. He hasn't been in contact for a while.'

'Are you concerned for his safety?' Lena asked bluntly.

'Not as concerned as you.'

'Are ASIS concerned for his safety?' Trig hesitated, and Lena drew a ragged breath. 'Trig? Tell me Jared's not working off the grid.'

'Can't tell you that.'

She put her hand to her head. 'But he *is* reporting to someone. To you.'

'No.'

'How long since anyone's seen him?'

'It's been a while.'

'Trig, how *long*?'

'Nineteen months.'

'What?' She didn't understand. Her confusion was visible, palpable, and so was her anxiety. He reached for her and she went to him, still trusting him as he wrapped his arms around her.

'How could we get married without him being there?' Her words were muffled by his chest but Trig heard them anyway. He could have come clean then. We're not married, he could have said.

But he didn't.

'Copper-haired girl said a woman and kid come in off that floating fortress once a week to attend a hospital appointment, regular as clockwork. They're due in today. Copper-haired girl said they come with bodyguards. There'll be someone to pilot the cruiser. I've tried to let Jared know we're here. Someone's clearing his phone messages. Might not be Jared, but if it is, he knows we're here and he'll do what he can to contact us.'

'You think he'll be part of the crew that's coming in today?'

'If he can be.'

'And if he's not?'

'I take you home. Come back alone. Try and get an invite aboard *Jericho3*.'

'No!' Lena's arms tightened around his waist. 'I'm not losing you too.'

'Lena—'

'*No*. If Jared can't get off that boat we put someone on watch here and we go home and pull Poppy and Damon into the picture and plan from there. You don't get to be the idiot my brother is. I won't let you.'

'God, I love the new you.' Trig lifted her and set her gently on the stone wall and she wrapped her legs around him and her arms around him as if she'd never let him go.

'Good, because I'm beginning to think that the old me was a fool.' Her eyes were grey this morning, a clear and guileless grey. 'I love you. These secrets you keep from me, they don't change that.'

He kissed her so that he wouldn't have to speak.

Because the secret he still held... The one that sat like acid in his gut...

That little revelation was primed to destroy both their worlds and he had no one to blame but himself.

TEN

——

'I don't like it,' Lena said at nine forty-five a.m. as they stood at the base of the eastern wall of Bodrum castle. Beyond the wall, a wharf teemed with tourists. Beyond that, a dozen tourist boats bobbed gently on the water.

'Plenty of cover,' said Trig. 'Lots of exits.'

'Lots of women and kids,' countered Lena grumpily. 'We don't know what kind of watercraft they'll be coming in on or when. What if we miss them?'

'The craft is going to be ocean-going, expensive, and the woman and kid have bodyguards. They won't be hard to spot, Lena. They're just not here yet.'

'I hate waiting,' she muttered. 'What time is it?'

'Nine-fifty.'

They'd been there since seven thirty, playing tourists, finding seats, taking pictures of the castle. The wharf was a beautiful, bustling place to have breakfast, but breakfast was long gone and nervousness was taking hold. 'I have a bad feeling about this,' she said. 'And I don't even know why. Something's off.' She looked up at Trig and didn't miss the swift flash of humour in his eyes. 'And don't say I don't have enough gut left to have gut instincts, because you're wrong. Half the touts here haven't taken their eyes off us for at least half an hour. They can ID us.'

'Why would they need to? We haven't done anything,' said Trig, and pulled her to her feet and slung his arm around her shoulder and guided her towards the tourist day boats—the ones that went out at ten and returned late in the afternoon. 'We're not *going* to do anything.'

Ten minutes later they'd reached the end of the wharf and there was still no sign of Jared. They stopped and looked out over the water. 'How's your leg?' asked Trig.

'Aches like a bitch.'

'And the rest of you?' Trig had a hand to the back of his neck and he would not meet her gaze. 'Does that ache too?'

'You mean from the sex?'

Trig cleared his throat and a slow flush crept up his neck. 'Yeah.'

'Those particular aches and pains were hard earned and I'm savouring every one of them,' she murmured. 'I can't believe I forgot how truly talented you are. Or how responsive.'

Trig looked as if he wanted to disappear. 'Hey,' she cajoled softly. 'I'm really sorry I couldn't remember any of it. I should have been able to, because it was mind-blowing. I'm saying this just in case you happen to have any performance anxiety left and in case it was connected to me not remembering our lovemaking. Trust me, your lovemaking is *not* something a woman would ever strive to forget.'

He laughed at that. A curt, embarrassed bark, cut short when his attention snagged on something out in the bay.

'What is it? Is it Jared?' Nineteen months since they'd last seen Jared, Trig had said, and all of a sudden Lena fiercely needed to see him and know that he was alive.

'Three hundred metres to the left of the tall ship,' murmured Trig. 'Six-seater orange power racer. Huge.'

Lena scanned the water for the vessel Trig had described and found it. 'Whoa. Not exactly hiding its light under a bushel, is it?'

'Please don't tell me you want one.'

'Couldn't afford it,' she said simply, for that was a billionaire's toy, no question. 'There's a kid in one of those seats.'

Trig nodded.

'I can't make out any faces.'

'Yet,' he said, and all of a sudden Lena desperately wanted one of those faces to belong to Jared. She wanted it with a ferocity that surprised her.

'Looks like it's heading for the far berths.' Lena wanted to hurry, but Trig was having none of it. He took her hand in his and swung her round to face him and waited until he had her full attention.

'Lena, you gave me your word that you only wanted to sight Jared and let him sight you. You promised me that you'd stay the hell out of whatever he's into.'

'I can't even remember that promise,' she snapped back.

'Then it's lucky I can.'

'Can we at least get a little closer?'

'Yes, but you need to stay close.'

'Done! Don't make me bruise you. C'mon.'

She pulled him forward and he came reluctantly. The powerboat drew closer. Four men, a woman and a kid.

'Pilot,' said Trig and the pilot was Jared, as darkly tanned and sinewy as she'd ever seen him. Lena stumbled and Trig shot out his hand to steady her.

'I'm okay,' she said faintly, but she didn't feel okay. Jared seemed to be aiming the boat for a berth at the very end of the wharf, a berth with a pier and a steel gate where the pier met the wharf. Trig made her stop short of it, still well within the tourist throng. Lena turned back towards the castle as Jared manoeuvred the cruiser closer, her eyes suddenly filled with tears. She couldn't even see Jared any more.

She wanted to scream at him, shake him for worrying them the way he had. For disappearing so completely. For blaming himself for her injuries.

Damn but her head hurt.

'Lena?' Trig said gruffly.

'I'm okay. Headache.' Every muscle in her body wanted to turn around so that her eyes could drink in the sight of Jared. It wasn't as if the boat wasn't stare worthy. Plenty of others would be looking at that beautiful superfast boat. She'd turn and look too. Soon. As soon as her tears went away. Damned if she'd let Jared see her crying. 'What are they doing?'

'Docking.'

'Who's getting off?'

'The woman and the kid. Two security types.'

'Not Jared?'

'No.'

'Has he seen you?' Trig was the most obvious one that Jared would look for. His size made him stand out.

'Yes.'

Lena turned, ignoring the stabbing pain behind one eye. She perused the boat, taking care to look impressed. It wasn't hard. And then she let her hungry gaze rest on Jared. He'd taken his sunglasses off and was using the hem of his T-shirt to clean them. He was looking straight at her.

'Go toss your water bottle in the bin over there,' Trig ordered gruffly. 'You wanted Jared to see you walking, so walk. Make sure he can see you.'

The words rang true. So true. Lena straightened and started towards the bin, smoothing out her gait as she went, trying to make walking seem effortless. 'Standing,' she wanted to say to her brother. 'Walking, you moron.' She tossed the empty bottle in the bin and turned so that the boat would come into view. Jared was watching her, a tiny smile tilting his lips. 'See?

I've done my part,' she wanted to say to him. 'Don't kill yourself doing yours. Matter of fact how about you get yourself home and give up this business of... this business of...'

Revenge.

Memory tugged at her, sharp and piercing, maddeningly out of reach. What the hell did any of this have to do with revenge?

Jared's passengers were just passing by, the security types lazily alert and carrying concealed, the woman digging in her purse and never breaking stride. The little boy looked straight at her, smiled and bent down to tie his shoelace. He didn't look sick. The woman stopped and looked back as if she'd sensed the disruption. 'Celik!' she said sharply, a name and a reprimand all tied up in a bow.

Celik stood and hurried to catch up to the woman. He didn't look back.

Neither of them looked back.

Lena looked to Jared and the other man in the boat. They were pulling away from the wharf, leaving, and she felt a swift tug of regret. She wanted her brother back within reach. Finding out who was responsible for her getting shot was all well and good, but not if it cost him his life and not if it meant him staying undercover for years.

'Let someone else go save the world,' she muttered and knew in that moment that she was done with ASIS, even if Jared wasn't. Even if Trig wasn't. She'd had enough.

Pain struck her just behind the eye again and she stopped and swayed and brought her fingers up to her forehead to try and chase it away. Blackness began to close in on her as her vision narrowed down to tunnels, the kind of tunnels that came with migraines, and all she wanted to do was get back to Trig and borrow some of his strength. Trig, who was her best friend and lover and...

Husband.

'God damn son of a bitch,' she muttered as knowledge slammed into her like a sucker punch.

Adrian Sinclair was many things to Lena but he wasn't her husband.

The proposal she hadn't been able to remember.

No wedding pictures to remind her of the big day.

The sex...

The sex.

She had barely enough time to glare at him; he'd barely taken half a dozen steps towards her before the world around her turned black.

Lena came to in Trig's arms, cradled to his chest. He was sitting on one of the benches scattered along the wharf. No humongous crowd surrounded them, and for that she was inordinately grateful.

She struggled up, out of his arms, and he let her go, but only as far as the space next to him on the seat. She smoothed back her hair and tried to make sense out of the jumble of memories crashing over her. 'I just—'

'Fainted,' said Trig, and handed her his half-full water bottle.

'For how long?'

'Couple of minutes.'

'Did Jared see?'

'Don't know, but he's gone. I caught you. There wasn't much fuss. Need to get you to the hospital here, though.'

'You planning on telling them you're my husband too?'

'You remember,' he said flatly.

Lena nodded slowly. 'Just then. Funny thing, memory loss. Bits and pieces kept coming back but not everything, not until I saw Jared and then they rushed back in like a tsunami. I remembered getting shot. I remembered you telling me to hold on. I remember waking up in the hospital in Darwin and everything else that came after... All the missing pieces, they slotted in as if they'd never been gone.'

'That's good,' he said.

'I still don't remember marrying you.'

Trig said nothing.

'We're not married, are we?'

'No.'

She nodded and twisted at her rings with clumsy fingers. She ducked her head because she didn't want him to see her cry. 'Why'd you let me believe that?'

'Your wallet was gone, you had no ID. I became your spouse at the hospital to get you treated faster.

I didn't realise you actually believed we were married until we got back to the hotel.'

'Why didn't you tell me then?'

'I didn't want to worry you. I wanted to protect you. I also thought that you'd most likely wake up the next morning and remember everything.'

'You lied to me.'

Trig nodded.

'I *trusted* you.'

'You still can.'

'*How?* You let me make a fool of myself with you! You *encouraged* it.'

'Is that what you think?'

'What else am I supposed to think?' She wrenched the rings off her finger and they sat there in her palm, shining dully. 'You let me believe in these.'

'You said you wanted them.'

'I was delusional. How could you let me believe in something that wasn't real?'

'It wasn't like that.'

'I was there. It was exactly like that.' The rings sat in her hand, softly gleaming. All she had to do was tilt her hand and they'd fall to the ground, but he wrapped his big hand around hers and gently closed her fingers over the rings.

'I'm sorry,' he said.

'You should be.' She wrenched her hand away. 'I trusted you. I *bedded* you. And you *let* me!'

'You made it difficult for me not to.'

'Oh, so it's *my* fault.'

'No. The fault's all mine.' He ran his hand over his face. 'I know I should have put you on a plane back to Australia the minute the doctor declared you fit to fly. I didn't. I brought you here instead in the hope that you could have a moment with your brother and see for yourself that he was okay. It's why you came to Turkey. It's the only reason you came here. I know that some of the decisions I've made over these past few days haven't been good ones, but I made that decision for you. I knew it would mean another night with you, but I honestly thought I could handle it.'

'Handle me.'

'I should have known better.' Trig's eyes beseeched her to listen. 'It wasn't all lies, Lena. I *want* that kind of relationship with you. My ring on your finger. You taking life in both hands and racing speedboats because it excites you and because you can. The farmhouse on the banks of the lazy river. The whole damn fantasy.'

'Maybe you do.' Lena's eyes began to fill with tears again. 'Doesn't give you the right to just reach out and *take* it.'

'Or we could dial it back a notch or two and you could agree to go out with me.'

She laughed at that. A bubbling, stumbling hiccough at his audacity. 'I *trusted* you.'

'You still can.'

'No.' She took his hand in hers and tipped the rings into his palm. She carefully closed his fingers around them and then withdrew from him altogether. She brought her knees to her chest and put her head to her knees, blocking out the world around them but the pain of betrayal stayed with her. 'I can't.'

On the subject of Lena going to the hospital, Trig stood unmoveable. Upon hearing of her recent concussion, the medical staff decided to monitor her overnight. Trig brought in clothes and toiletries. He called her family and gave them the happenings of the day. He changed their flights and had the Istanbul doctor forward her medical records on to this new hospital. He took control. Quietly. Efficiently. He didn't pretend to be her husband.

'I'm feeling okay,' Lena told him when the nurse came in to tell him that visiting hours were over and that Lena needed her rest. 'I honestly think I'm fine now. He's leaving.'

'No lie. I'm feeling okay,' Lena repeated as the nurse withdrew from the room. Tension hung there between them, a tension built on all the things they hadn't said these past few hours. He'd helped her find Jared, and that was worth something. But he'd betrayed her trust too, and that hurt; God, it hurt. A nameless stranger had put a spray of bullets in her gut and almost destroyed her. This man had put a bullet straight through her heart.

'I want to thank you for today,' she began. 'Jared's alive and I know that now. I've seen him and he's seen me. Whatever he's doing... I can't stop him from doing it. He wants to save the world, one bad guy at a time, and that's a noble ambition. It's just not my ambition any more. Mine are smaller now. Right now I just want to get through the day without falling apart emotionally. I always have had an emo streak.'

'You're doing fine,' he said gruffly.

'No. I'm not. I need you to not be here any more. I need you to hear what I'm saying. You should go home.'

When visiting hours came around the next morning, Poppy was there for her.

And Trig was not.

ELEVEN

—

Five days later, Lena was back at Damon's beach house by the sea and Poppy—who'd escorted her there—had headed back to Darwin and the delicious Sebastian who'd claimed Poppy's heart. Poppy hadn't pried, when it came to what had happened between Lena and Trig in Turkey. Poppy had been relieved to know that Jared was alive, and more relieved still when the doctor had discharged Lena and given her the all-clear to travel. Jared was busy doing whatever it was he was doing, and that was his idiot decision and no one else's, as far as Poppy was concerned.

'*Now* will you let it go and concentrate on living your life?' Poppy had said as they'd packed their bags for home. 'Because it's right there in front of you and it's ready when you are.'

Five days since Lena had told Trig to go.

And the loneliness and sense of *wrong* ate away at her soul.

She had everything she needed here at Damon's house. Comfort and space and a gorgeous indoor pool. So many pools in her life, only now she remembered why. The countless hours of water-based rehab. The agonising stretches as she regained the use of her left leg, one millimetre at a time, refusing to admit defeat. Damon had practically given over this house to her—no wonder she'd thought of it as hers. Hers and Trig's, because he'd spent almost as much time here as she had these past nineteen months. Babysitting her, she'd always thought. Encouraging her with his silence when others had told her to stop. Adding his strength of will to hers. Sometimes he'd even gone away when she'd yelled at him to leave her alone, but he'd never stayed gone for long. It wasn't his way. This time, though...

All bets were off.

Her mobile rang and Lena found it on the little table beside Damon's front door and looked at the screen in sudden trepidation, swiftly followed by a stab of disappointment. Not Trig. Ruby. Lena tapped the screen to answer the call and stood a little straighter because Ruby had that effect on people.

'I hear congratulations are in order,' she said lightly, for she hadn't yet congratulated Ruby on her pregnancy, and that was an oversight she wanted to fix. 'Congratulations.'

'Thank you. I told Damon I wanted to tell you in person but boys will be boys. Apparently he and Trig had nothing else to talk about on the phone the other day besides the fact that Trig was setting up a meeting with your brother and that somewhere along the line he'd fake married you. Which is, in fact, why I'm calling you. I hear you're still at odds with my second favourite man on the planet.'

'Ruby, are you cross examining me?'

'Would you like me to rephrase the question? What's going on, Lena? It's not like you to hold a grudge.'

'He let me think that we were on our honeymoon, Ruby. He lied to me. Over and over again. Who *does* that? To someone they supposedly care about?'

'You need to examine the event carefully,' said Ruby. 'Did he at any time *tell* you that you were on your honeymoon? Or did you assume it? Because maybe what happened was that you assumed it and Trig simply failed to correct you. Maybe the doctor had ordered rest for you. No strenuous activity or thinking too hard. Maybe Trig thought you'd sleep on it and wake up the next morning with your memories intact.'

'You're his defence lawyer, aren't you?'

'If I was I wouldn't be calling you. Your partial memory loss placed Trig in an extremely awkward situation. He did his best. He always does his best for you.'

'He lied to me. He let me make a fool out of myself. Ruby...' Lena bit back a sob '...I was so happy. I was planning all sorts of rubbish.'

'Like what?'

'A big old house for us to live in. Christmas decorations. Kids. I can't have kids. Didn't stop me saying yes to them. Adopted kids. Surrogate kids. I'm pretty sure we made plans to borrow your kids every now and again. We had it all worked out. I thought it was *real*. I bedded him. I thought it was real.'

'Trig *slept* with you?'

'Yes.'

'Poor Trig.'

'Poor *Trig*? What about poor me?'

'He knew you'd find out that you weren't married to him sooner or later. He figured that as long as the marriage sham didn't go too far and that you got to see Jared, everything would work out for the best in the long run. Your needs before his, and all that. How *did* you get him to bed you, by the way? Because the last time I spoke to him that was definitely not part of the plan. On pain of death not part of the plan.'

'Oh, you know me.' Lena closed her eyes and rubbed at her temple. 'I badger and bully and prey on people's weaknesses and generally don't take no for an answer.'

'I'm relatively sure that's not true,' said Ruby carefully.

'You weren't there.'

'So you're *not* blaming Trig for that part of the mess.'

'Oh, no. I still am. He's a great target for anger. I think it's those broad shoulders. It's just…maybe I'm okay with blaming me too. Doesn't make anything *right*.'

'No, but it's a start,' Ruby offered gently. 'Here's what you're going to do. You're going to make a coffee or a tea, and then you're going to sit down and draw up two columns. The first column is what happened in Turkey. Stick to the facts. The second column is what you want to happen now.'

'What about what Trig wants to happen?'

'Add another column. Get him to fill it out. You *do* know that he's stupidly in love with you? You're not second-guessing that?'

'I am second-guessing that. I look in the mirror and there's so much of me there that's not pretty. Inside and out. I don't know what he sees in me.'

'Soul mate, kindred spirit, partner in crime...'

'I can't do those things that we used to do.'

'May I draw your attention back to column two?' Ruby said patiently. 'In it you put all the things that you can do, want to do and dream of doing with the man you call Trig.'

'That's another three columns.'

'Have it your way. Call me tomorrow if you get stuck. Call Trig tomorrow too. Don't blame yourself, or him, for a situation that neither of you had much control over. Do take control of the situation you're in now.'

'Are you sure you're a lawyer and not a psychotherapist?'

'Sometimes you have to be both.'

Lena paused. Ruby was part of this family now. A strong and savvy woman with a lot of good times and bad behind her. The kind of woman a person could rely on. 'May I really call you if I need more help with this?'

'Any time.'

'Thanks. Tell Damon hello.'

'Will do.' Ruby hung up. Lena put her phone back on the table. Weariness washed over her as she made her way to the couch. Being off her feet and horizontal beckoned. Memories of Trig beckoned too. Of him in a Turkish bath house, valiantly trying to preserve her modesty. Of him talking starry nights and turtles. Of Lena dancing in his arms while a pianola played softly in the background. Of Trig stripped naked and loving her.

Say it.

Trig loves me.

Again.

You do know that he's stupidly in love with you.

Trig loves me.

Again.

Two minutes later, she was asleep.

Adrian Sinclair had never been one for inactivity. Waiting drove him crazy. Waiting for word from a woman who'd already driven him crazy merely doubled the crazy. He couldn't sit still. He couldn't sleep. Work didn't hold his interest. Physical activity leading to exhaustion couldn't stem his agitation. For the last three nights he'd gone to bed exhausted and woken up dreaming of Lena. Replaying in his head what he should have done or could have done.

And hadn't.

He knew Lena was home now. She'd arrived home with Poppy the day before yesterday. Poppy had called. Lena hadn't. Ruby had called. Lena hadn't. Trig's father had called, and Trig had asked him what kind of price old farmhouses on the banks of a lazy river were going for.

His father had asked him what he'd been drinking, but he'd been drinking nothing, nothing at all.

And Lena still hadn't called.

Adrian Sinclair had always gone after what he wanted, sometimes with excruciating single-mindedness. Unless one was talking about the indomitable Lena West. Trig had barely gone after Lena at all. He'd been waiting for the right time, the right place, the right blasted moon in the sky.

He was done waiting. He needed a plan of attack, a plan to make Lena respond to him again the way she'd responded to him in Turkey. She'd been happy with him once. All he had to do was make that happen again. He could fight dirty. He could fight hard. Why wait?

He hated waiting.

By the time Trig arrived home from work that afternoon he had a plan. By the time he'd opened his emails and seen the picture of the old homestead that his father had sent him, he had a better plan. He dialled Lena's number but she didn't pick up. Half an hour later he dialled it again. This time she must have had it with her, because she answered on the third ring.

'Do you remember what I made you repeat back to me when we were making love in the crazy room?' he began without preamble.

'*What?*'

'Say it. Say Trig loves me and always will.'

'I'm not a parrot.'

She sounded frustrated. He could handle a frustrated Lena. He'd been doing so for the past two years. It wasn't as if he'd been expecting a declaration of undying devotion from her or even a simple 'I've missed you'. But she *had* told him she'd loved him not so long ago, and he held to that the way a free soloing climber so often held to a rock face.

By his fingertips.

'Okay, so I lied to you about us being married. I should have come clean and I didn't and I ended up with one foot in heaven and the other one in hell. You gave me a glimpse of what we *could* have if we dropped the barriers and simply let ourselves be what we wanted to be. Like married, for example. We could make that happen. Everything we talked about we could make happen if we wanted it to.'

She had no comeback for him beyond a strangled sound that he hoped to hell wasn't a sob.

'I love you, Lena. I always will. Check your emails.'

He hung up on her after that. He sent her the picture of the old homestead his father had sent him and the links to the 'For Sale' information. He attached his father's rough estimate of what it would cost to make it habitable.

'Where's the river?' she emailed back, some ten minutes later.

He didn't wait ten minutes to reply. 'Below the hill. It's a mostly lazy river prone to brief yet frenzied flooding. That's why the house is on the hill.'

She didn't write back.

Trig decided not to think of her lack of response as defeat. She'd answered his call and she'd answered his email and it was a start. He'd never thought that winning Lena's forgiveness was going to be easy. He didn't want easy. He'd never courted that.

He wanted Lena.

The next morning, before work, he emailed her links to a bunch of mosaic tile manufacturers. For the bath-house floor, he wrote. And left it at that.

She called him that evening when he was on his way home from work.

'I need help filling out a form,' she said.

'What kind of form?'

'There's three columns. Column one is what happened to us in Turkey, otherwise known as "The Facts" column. Column two is what I want to happen from here on in. Column three is what you want to happen. It was Ruby's idea.'

'I love that woman.'

'You say that a lot. You can understand my confusion.'

'I love you more.'

Lena sighed. 'May I send you the form?'

'Have you filled out your column yet?'

'I filled out the first two columns. It took me two days.'

'What if I don't agree with The Facts?'

'Feel free to amend them. Ruby said you might want to. Something about reframing.'

'Smart woman.'

Silence filled the car.

'You're smart too,' he added hastily. 'I know that.'

'It's probably better if you don't talk,' she said, and hung up.

Trig made it home in record time and only marginally exceeded the speed limit. He grabbed his personal laptop from the floor beside the couch, carried it through to the kitchen and sat it next to last night's empty pizza box. He opened it up and switched it on. He grabbed a cola from the fridge and waited for his computer to wake up completely. He grabbed a stool, sat on it and started jiggling his leg. He vowed to get a faster computer along with a speedier Internet service. He hated waiting. Finally, he found Lena's email and opened it up. She hadn't bothered with an introduction. She'd started with column one.

The Facts:
1)*Lena loves Trig (and not like a brother). Romantically. Inescapably. No one else has ever measured up to him. Not even close.*

Trig hadn't been aware of this fact until now and snorted cola up his nose and then all over the counter on account of it. But he was totally on board with this fact. He read it again, just to make sure he'd read it right before moving on to fact number two.

2)*Trig loves Lena.*

No surprises there.

3)*Everyone but Lena and Trig knows that Lena loves Trig and that Trig loves Lena (this fact has been substantiated by Ruby, Poppy, Poppy's Seb, Damon and Damon on Jared's behalf).*

Some people were so smug.

4)*Lena and Trig went to Istanbul to find Jared. They found him.*

Nothing but the facts.

5)Lena fell and hit her head, lost her memory and thought she was married to Trig.

True.

6)Trig let her believe that she was married to him.

Loaded word, 'let'. It implied some semblance of control.

7)Lena wanted to bed Trig.

Trig grinned in spite of himself and downed half a can of cola, this time without getting it up his nose.

8)Trig resisted.

'Yes, I did. And it wasn't exactly easy.'

9)Lena still wanted to bed Trig.

Trig *liked* these facts.

10) Trig resisted. Some might call that chivalrous. Lena found it frustrating.

'Try being me.'

11)Lena seduced Trig.

That was one interpretation.

12)Trig let her.

He really thought she was misusing the word 'let'. He wanted a new word. One that described active participation.

13)Lena saw Jared, regained her memory, realised she wasn't married to Trig and got confused and angry.

Succinct.

14)Lena thought she might have coerced Trig into something he didn't want.

'What?' When had he *ever* given her the impression that he didn't know exactly what he wanted? Namely her. Unless she was talking about those times during those first few nights when she'd wanted him to be cosy with her and he hadn't...and then later when she'd wanted a wedding night to remember and he'd developed a fondness for long showers and a predilection for performance anxiety... Okay, so maybe she had a point. But surely proclaiming his love for her before, during and *after* her memory loss had to count for something?

15)Lena thought Trig might have coerced her into something she didn't want. She didn't know what to think and she didn't know what was real.

'Figure it out,' he begged her. 'Believe.'

16)Lena temporarily ignored the fact that she loves Trig and Trig loves her and that they could probably work something out.

That was the end of The Facts according to Lena. Trig ran a shaky hand across his face. There were some high points, sure. The first two points and the last. Love. Remarkable things could happen in the presence of love. But there'd been some low points too. Sighing, Trig moved on to the next column.

What Lena Wants:
1)Lena has never really thought about what she wants.

Not helpful, Lena.

2)She followed Trig and Jared into the special intelligence service because it seemed like a good fit for her and because she wanted to maintain her connec-

tion with them. Her heart wasn't always in the job but she was with Jared and Trig so she was mostly happy.

Trig frowned. Thinking that Lena needed to reconsider her options on account of her recent physical limitations was one thing. Having Lena admit that she'd never been completely on board with a career in special intelligence was quite another. Sure, it was good news in the overall scheme of things *now*, but you'd think he might have noticed. Or that Jared might have noticed. Why the hell hadn't anyone noticed that her heart wasn't in it? *Mostly happy.* What the hell was that?

3)Working for ASIS doesn't seem like such a good fit for Lena any more.

Trig agreed. She could do a lot better than mostly happy.

4)Lena needs a new career. She's considering becoming a physiotherapist to people with mobility issues, or a psychotherapist to people with mobility issues, or both.

He could see her doing that.

5)She has the money to go back to school and study. Lena likes study, even if study doesn't always like her.

Lena was smart. Maybe not as smart as her siblings, Jared excluded, but few people were. Trig had no doubt that Lena would accomplish whatever she set out to do. She never gave up. Even when the odds were stacked against her. He loved that about her. He always had.

6)In her spare time, Lena will race speedboats. Should Lena and Trig acquire two speedboats, Lena will race the red one.

Trig laughed.

7)Lena wants to marry Trig.

Trig's heart kicked hard against his chest.

8)And live in a farmhouse high on a hill above the banks of a lazy and occasionally crazy river. And help raise his babies, adopted babies and possibly a couple of puppies. Lena wants the children to call her Mum and the dogs to think she's the boss.

Trig ran a rough hand across his face. Everything he'd ever wanted was right here in column two. Mainly because everything he'd ever wanted had always led back to Lena.

9)She also wants a Turkish bathing pool built somewhere inside the farmhouse. This pool will have water spouts, waterfalls and marble ledges to lie on.

Fortunately she didn't want a eunuch with that.

10)Lena still wants Jared home so that she can kick his arse for not keeping in touch—but that can wait.
11)Lena wants to work around her physical limitations rather than resent them. She may need to be reminded of this from time to time.

Damn, but he loved this woman.

12)Lena wants Trig. Repeat: Lena wants Trig and wants to know what he wants so that she can adjust her plans accordingly. Compromise is in her vocabulary. She looked it up in the Wiktionary.

The third column, 'What Trig Wants', stood ominously blank. The cut and paste option had never been more tempting. Instead, Trig opened up a new file and prepared to give his future some serious thought.

Half an hour and half a dozen words later, Trig decided that he was a man of action rather than words.

Fifteen minutes after that he was in the car, heading for Damon's beach house and Lena.

Lena woke to the sound of someone pounding impatiently on Damon's front door. She squinted at the bedside clock and groaned. Five twenty-two a.m. She'd waited up last night until almost one a.m. Waiting for a reply from Trig that had never come. He hadn't emailed or called. She'd finally caved and called him, only to find that his phone was out of range or turned off. Why hadn't he called? Because he wasn't mean like that. Thoughtless on occasion, yes, but never mean. Lena's eyes drifted closed.

And the pounding started again and this time her brain kicked into gear and she sat bolt upright. Who *else* would be at her door at five-something a.m.?

Her body didn't want to hurry down Damon's long hallway but where there was a will there was a way and Lena made it to the door in record time. She unbolted it and opened it and there stood Trig, his smile brighter than the sun. The dark stubble on his face and the rumpled business shirt minus tie only added to his appeal.

'I brought croissants,' he said. 'They're still hot.'

Lena had to move to see past him, but eventually she spotted his car. 'You drove here overnight?'

'It's not that far.'

'How much coffee did you have?'

'I lost count,' he murmured and dropped a kiss on

her unprotesting lips as he sailed past her. 'Consider me wide awake.'

He headed for the kitchen, Lena followed. 'You drove here,' she said again.

'The planes were too slow.'

'So you drove here.'

'You're not quite as awake as me, are you?'

Guess not.

'You said you loved me. In an *email*,' he continued as if she'd just shredded his favourite kite sail. 'I've decided to forgive you for that, by the way, but I needed to be here in person to give you my reply. Because that's how it's done. *In person*.'

'Oh.' Lena tried to hide her smile. She leaned against the kitchen counter with her hands trapped between her back and the counter, because if she reached for him they wouldn't talk and he sounded like he needed to talk. 'I thought I'd *already* told you that I loved you in person,' she offered dulcetly. 'I remember it distinctly. It was right after you proposed the second time. Or was it the first? Or does that time not count because I thought we were already married and you knew we weren't.'

'It counts.' Trig scowled.

Lena smiled.

'For someone who looks so angelic, you're really good at torture,' he muttered.

'You love it,' she said. 'You love me.'

'I do.' Trig reached behind him and pulled from his

pocket a crumpled sheet of paper. He unfolded it and it turned into two crumpled sheets of paper. 'It's your list of what you want.'

'Where's yours?'

In my head. He scanned the paper. Nodded a couple of times.

'I don't want to quit ASIS,' he said. 'I may even want to take the occasional field job. When the kids arrive I aim to retire from fieldwork and carve out a place for myself in operations review. Turns out I'm good at it. That okay by you?'

'Yes.' Just because she didn't want a man as careless with his life as Jared was, didn't mean she wanted a placid man who played everything safe. 'That'll work.'

'Good.' He returned his attention to the paper in his hand. 'I have a couple of adjustments to make to the poolside plans. I want Turkish tile trim, a retractable roof and a marble mermaid on the steps. And fairy lights.'

'Because, why not?' she murmured.

'Exactly. And much as I want Jared at my wedding, I'm not going to wait another nineteen months for him to come home. I say we send him an invite to our June wedding and see if he turns up.'

'June, you say. Okay.' She could be a winter bride. 'Give him an exit date to aspire to.'

'Puppies,' Trig said next, and Lena smiled at his priorities. 'I want to get them from the pound and they must, when grown, stand at least knee high. I will train the puppies not to crush the children. All children and puppies will think I'm the boss.'

'You always did like a challenge.'

'So true. I want to honeymoon at Saul's Caravan, and this time we'll do it right.'

'Perfect,' said Lena.

Trig tossed the paper on the counter and stepped in close, his hands either side of her, his eyes smiling as he pressed his lips to the curve of her mouth. 'Do I need to propose to you again?'

'I think you do.'

'You want the moon and the stars again?'

'And the turtles. And Saturn's rings.'

'I knew you liked that one best.'

'Well, you always remember your first.'

She wound her arms around his neck and kissed him, then. Savouring him. Loving him. She reached for the topmost button of his shirt and undid it. She undid the second button for him too.

'I love you, Lena.'

'I know,' she whispered and brought her hands up to frame his face. 'And you're right. Saying it to the person in person is better, so... Adrian Trig Sinclair, I love you too.'

TWELVE

——

Six months later...

Lena couldn't reach the zip on her dress. Fortunately, that was what bridesmaids were for. Poppy and Ruby fussed and tweaked until the silk and tulle sweetheart gown sat perfectly on Lena's skin, unashamedly romantic with its fitted beaded bodice and floor-length tulle skirt. Lena had chosen the gown, with Poppy and Ruby's full approval. Ruby had chosen the shoes and the hair accessories, because, frankly, when you had an expert in the family it paid to stand back and let them do what they did best.

The wedding shoes were amber-whorled white sling-backs. The headband involved an elegant sufficiency of tiny gumnuts and delicate white flannel flowers, perfect for an outdoor wedding that would shortly take place beneath a towering redgum on the banks of a lazy river.

Ruby and her baby belly glowed in a moss-green

full-length gown with an empire waist. Poppy's dress ran along similar lines except that hers was a pale sky-blue. The old farmhouse bedroom that currently doubled as the dressing room had been finished and furnished last week—an early wedding gift from Lena's soon-to-be father-in-law. The bed was custom made and enormous. The freshly waxed floorboards had come from fallen timber, sourced on the farm. The silk carpets that covered large sections of floorboards had come from Persia. Lena had bought them at auction three weeks earlier and hiding them from Trig had required great stealth and the assistance of a recently rebuilt chimney.

Trig had wanted to light a fire in the fireplace last night.

Yeah, no.

Not until Damon and Seb had dragged Trig to the other end of the property to cut firewood, leaving Lena, Ruby and Poppy to shift the damn things.

Ruby was six months pregnant with twins, Lena had a gammy leg and Poppy had been too busy laughing to be of much help at all, but between the three of them they'd hauled the carpets into one of the shower stalls in an unfinished bathroom, and Trig's brother and father had laid them out in the master bedroom this morning.

Lena hoped Trig loved them.

If he didn't, she could always send him out shopping for more.

'Half an hour until go time,' said Poppy, and Lena

looked out of the big bay window towards the lawn where the after-the-ceremony celebrations would take place. A marquee had been set up on the garden lawn. Inside, a trio of waiters offered liquid refreshments to arriving guests. Parasols, picnic rugs and fluffy beach towels had been made available for the more intrepid guests who wanted to explore the river banks or the river itself. Caterers had taken over the kitchen. Long trestle tables had appeared on the lawn, covered in white linen tablecloths, shiny silverware and white accompaniments. The florist and her assistants were putting the final touches to the table arrangements. The bridal bouquets waited on the sideboard, a romantic mass of flannel flowers, gumnuts and soft green leaves.

A pair of vintage Aston Martin DB9s stood waiting in the circular driveway, ready to take first Ruby and Poppy and then Lena and her father down the freshly levelled track from the house to the redgum by the river where the wedding would take place. One of the Astons was silver, the other a British racing green. Together, they put Lena in mind of fast men and reckless women. They were a gift to her and Trig from her father.

Trig didn't know they owned the Astons yet, or that twice a year at a racetrack in Brisbane enthusiasts still raced the things. Good times ahead.

The photographer tried to be unobtrusive as she took stills of them getting ready. The photographer had already been out and taken photos of the cars.

'What have I forgotten?' Lena knew she was almost ready, but not quite.

'Jewellery,' said Poppy, with the click of her fingers, and reached for a tired velvet case that she nonetheless treated with reverence. They'd belonged to their mother.

Gently, Poppy helped her put them on.

'Beautiful,' said Ruby, suddenly misty eyed.

'Perfect,' said Poppy.

Lena's wedding planner stuck her head around the door, her eyes bright and her smile reassuring. 'How are we going?'

'She's ready,' said Poppy.

'Good. The musicians are here and they're all set up, the caterer wants to take your kitchen with him wherever he goes and the groom and his party have been spotted. They're down by the river.'

'Hopefully not getting wet,' Ruby muttered.

'There was some mention of a speedboat,' the wedding planner replied carefully. 'A very fast speedboat. Apparently they arrived in one.'

'Fancy that.' Lena grinned. She hadn't had time to go speedboat shopping, what with finding and buying the farm and getting it restored and enrolling in university and planning a wedding. Perhaps Trig had.

The only blight on her otherwise perfect day was the absence of Jared. By all accounts he was still on the floating fortress belonging to the billionaire arms dealer. 'I wish Jared was here.' There, she'd said it.

'His loss,' said Ruby gently.

'Damn right it is.' But it still stung and not just on her account. She hurt on Trig's behalf too.

'He'd have been here if he could have,' Poppy said defensively.

Or if he'd wanted to. But Lena kept that thought to herself. No point focusing on the negatives. She'd stopped doing that, for the most part. Joy ruled her now, along with gratitude for what was. Happiness did that. And love. Love made so many things possible.

The wedding planner checked her phone and smiled some more. 'Your father's here. He's out by the cars. We've scheduled ten minutes for photos. Twenty minutes until we leave for the river bank.'

It wasn't that far. Most of the guests had opted to walk down the hill from the homestead to the river bank.

The photographer nodded and made her exit. Poppy handed Lena the bridal bouquet.

Together, Ruby and Poppy floated the bridal veil over Lena's head.

'You look so beautiful,' said Poppy.

'You do.' Ruby nodded. 'Hope suits you. Happiness suits you.'

'Are you ready?' asked Poppy and Lena nodded.

Yes, she was.

Trig hated waiting. He especially hated waiting in front of three hundred or so guests for his bride to turn up, but he made the most of it and greeted people, right up until Damon's phone buzzed and a text message from Ruby told them Lena was on her way.

Damon herded him and Trig's brother Matthew, his best man, beneath the redgum, where they waited some more.

A dark green Aston Martin appeared on the track down to the river. A silver one followed.

'Nice,' said Matthew.

'Very nice,' agreed Damon, and turned to Trig and straightened the little white flannel flower on his lapel. 'Also a wedding gift. My father said to tell you that one of them's yours and that the green one's marginally faster. Welcome to the family.'

'Thanks. I think.' Trig could barely breathe as Poppy and Ruby emerged from the first car and then helped Lena and her father exit the second. They fussed and they fiddled and generally took for ever.

'Something's wrong,' he said.

'No, I'm pretty sure it's normal,' said Matthew.

'It's normal,' said the celebrant. 'They're waiting for the music.'

Right. The music.

Solo guitar, and it started right on cue.

Poppy lined up in the walkway between the ancient fallen gums that doubled as pews. Ruby moved into place behind her. Then Lena and her father began to head his way. Lena looked so beautiful, so fragile, but she wasn't fragile at all. She was the keeper of his heart and she held it with the same strength and determination that she brought to everything else.

'Breathe,' prompted his brother and Trig remembered to breathe.

And then Lena was upon him, with Poppy and Ruby beside her as her father moved away.

'Dearly beloved,' began the celebrant, and Trig felt himself relax a fraction. This was real. It was really happening.

The thrum of a fast-moving speedboat reached his ears. A really fast-moving speedboat. The celebrant frowned and glanced towards the river.

'Dearly beloved,' he said again, only now just about everyone's attention was turned towards the river, including Lena's. Trig looked too as the speedboat came into view from around the bend. He narrowed his eyes, because the boat looked strangely familiar. As in almost exactly the same as the one he'd arrived in except that the one he'd arrived in was black and this one was red.

'Trig,' said Lena, in a voice that was nowhere near calm. 'Is that maniac driving the boat *Jared*? Because it sure as hell looks like Jared.'

It *was* Jared, Trig decided. And Trig was going to kill him. 'Did you know about this?' he barked at Damon. 'Did you know he was on his way? And you didn't tell us?'

'No!' Damon held up his hands. 'No. Not my fault. Or my doing. You were the one who texted him the invitation.'

'Did *any* of you know?' Trig's voice was dangerously calm.

But the answers all came back no.

'Could be his evil twin,' said Damon helpfully.

'You wished him here,' Poppy told Lena solemnly, right before she dissolved into helpless giggles.

Matthew turned to the crowd and held up his hands. 'We're taking a five-minute break, people.'

Lena's father came to stand with them and so did Seb. Trig drew a steadying breath. Five minutes wasn't so long. And then he'd be married. He watched in tight-lipped silence as Jared kept that boat at full throttle until cutting the engine at the very last minute and swinging the craft in behind Trig's. Jared missed the other boat by at least an inch.

'And you wanted him here why?' murmured Ruby.

Excellent question.

And then Jared climbed from the boat and strode confidently towards them. Only his eyes gave him away, because they were pleading and wary and long past exhausted. An angry graze ran the length of his face. The less said about his jeans and filthy T-shirt, the better.

'You didn't RSVP,' said Lena tightly. Lena looked as if she was about to cry.

'But I did get here.' Jared silently pleaded with her for understanding before turning his battered face towards Trig. 'Honoured to be your groomsman, man. Did you really think I was going to miss this one?'

'You stole my boat. My *other* boat. Lena's boat.'

'Pity he couldn't have stolen a suit to go with it,' muttered Ruby.

'I don't believe we've met,' said Jared, straightening fast, his eyes straying to Ruby's big belly.

Damon stepped up and offered the introductions. 'Ruby, Jared. Jared, Ruby. Ruby's my wife.'

'You did manage to miss that one,' offered Ruby.

'I'm Seb,' said Sebastian, shrugging out of his jacket and handing it to Jared, who got with the programme fast and slipped it on. 'I'm here with Poppy. We're not married. Yet.'

Jared's eyes grew sharp fast. He held out his hand and Seb shook it. Hand crushing ensued.

'This isn't at all how I imagined this would go,' said Poppy, leaning forward and frowning at both Jared and Seb.

'Never assume,' offered Jared.

'Trig?' Lena's voice wobbled, he could hear it wobbling and the notion that she might be having second thoughts focused him the way nothing else could.

'What do you need?' Behind him, Seb and Lena's father melted away and his groomsmen fell silently into line, first his brother then Jared and then Damon.

'Can we ignore them and get married now?' Her voice still wobbled.

'I'm ignoring them. I can't even see them. There's only you.' He closed his fingers over hers and brought her fingers up to his lips.

The celebrant smiled and started again. 'Dearly beloved...'

Five minutes later, the friends and families that had gathered beneath a big old redgum tree by the banks of a lazy river cheered, clapped, whistled and hollered with delight.

As first the bride and then the groom said I Do.

* * * * *

REQUEST YOUR FREE BOOKS!
2 FREE NOVELS PLUS 2 FREE GIFTS!

YES! Please send me 2 FREE Harlequin® Kiss novels and my 2 FREE gifts (gifts worth about $10). After receiving them, if I don't wish to receive any more books, I can return the shipping statement marked "cancel." If I don't cancel, I will receive 4 brand-new novels every month and be billed just $4.30 per book in the U.S. or $4.99 per book in Canada. That's a savings of at least 13% off the cover price! It's quite a bargain! Shipping and handling is just 50¢ per book in the U.S. and 75¢ per book in Canada.* I understand that accepting the 2 free books and gifts places me under no obligation to buy anything. I can always return a shipment and cancel at any time. Even if I never buy another book, the two free books and gifts are mine to keep forever.

145/345 HDN FVXQ

Name	(PLEASE PRINT)

Address	Apt. #

City	State/Prov.	Zip/Postal Code

Signature (if under 18, a parent or guardian must sign)

Mail to the **Harlequin® Reader Service:**
IN U.S.A.: P.O. Box 1867, Buffalo, NY 14240-1867
IN CANADA: P.O. Box 609, Fort Erie, Ontario L2A 5X3

Want to try two free books from another line?
Call 1-800-873-8635 or visit www.ReaderService.com.

* Terms and prices subject to change without notice. Prices do not include applicable taxes. Sales tax applicable in N.Y. Canadian residents will be charged applicable taxes. Offer not valid in Quebec. This offer is limited to one order per household. Not valid for current subscribers to Harlequin Kiss books. All orders subject to credit approval. Credit or debit balances in a customer's account(s) may be offset by any other outstanding balance owed by or to the customer. Please allow 4 to 6 weeks for delivery. Offer available while quantities last.

Your Privacy—The Harlequin® Reader Service is committed to protecting your privacy. Our Privacy Policy is available online at www.ReaderService.com or upon request from the Harlequin Reader Service.

We make a portion of our mailing list available to reputable third parties that offer products we believe may interest you. If you prefer that we not exchange your name with third parties, or if you wish to clarify or modify your communication preferences, please visit us at www.ReaderService.com/consumerschoice or write to us at Harlequin Reader Service Preference Service, P.O. Box 9062, Buffalo, NY 14269. Include your complete name and address.

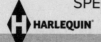
Inventing a fake fiancé was an act of desperation
for Zoe Montgomery—a knee-jerk response to
her horrifying high school reunion! But now that
she's convinced London's most unattainable
bachelor to play the part, her little white lie is
spiraling out of control!

"So that's the deal, Zoe. One kiss. Take it or leave it."

Well, what option did she have under the circumstances but
to agree? she thought, caving in to the common sense she usually
valued so highly but seemed to have abandoned tonight.

It had better be one hell of a kiss, though. Just the thought
of having his mouth on hers, properly this time, was making
her heart thump and her knees wobble.

"Okay, well, fine," she said, feeling all hot and tingly again
at the prospect of the two of them kissing. "But could you at
least try to make it look convincing?"

Taking her hand and tugging her toward a gap in the
crowds, where they'd have maximum exposure, Dan shot her
a quick, smoldering smile. "I'll do my best."

Zoe's instant, scorchingly hot response to him—the way
she melted into him with a soft sigh, the tightening of her

arms around his neck and the pressure of her pelvis tilting up against his, and then the little moans she started making at the back of her throat—was mind-blowing, and within seconds the kiss had taken on a life of its own.

He'd never had a kiss quite like this. He'd never had his mind go quite so blank quite so fast. He'd never had the feeling that the world around him was disintegrating. And he'd never experienced such a swift rush of desire, such instant heat, nor such a reckless longing to toss aside his control and give in to such clamoring raw need.

Who knew where the intensity of it came from, the insanely desperate urge to flatten Zoe against the nearest suitable surface and get her naked. Whatever it was—and really, his brain was in no state to try to work it out—Dan didn't want the kiss to end.

And it might not have, had a distant wolf whistle, followed by a suggestion they get a room, not sliced through the fog in his head and brought him thumping down to earth.

Reluctantly drawing back, he stared down at the woman in his arms. Her eyes were glazed, her cheeks were pink and her lips were rosy from the pressure of the kiss, and her breathing was all ragged and shallow. She looked as shaken as he felt, and at the realization that she'd been as affected as he had, his self-control rocked for a second. He could still feel every inch of her pressed up against him, was achingly aware of her breasts crushed to his chest, and all he could think about was doing it again.

Don't miss this scandalous new romance!
THE REUNION LIE by Lucy King

Available December 2013, only from
Harlequin® KISS!

Her million-dollar question!

AVAILABLE NOVEMBER 19, 2013!

THE MOST EXPENSIVE NIGHT OF HER LIFE

by Amy Andrews

Supermodel Ava Kelly is more used to luxury yachts than London canal boats. But she desperately needs a refuge from the paparazzi, and delectable Blake Walker's boat will provide the perfect bolt-hole. This brooding ex-soldier is bound to rescue her, right...?

Wrong. Pampered princess Ava is the last person Blake wants in his personal space—she's far too tempting! But with a million-dollar charity donation hanging in the balance, Blake can't say no. Now that Ava's close enough to touch, keeping his hands off her is pretty difficult, too! Maybe money isn't the only thing at stake this Christmas....